BIBLIOGRAPHY

The Dash Hammond Series:

The Price of Being Neighborly
The Cost of Kindness
The Expense of Family
A Wealth of Women
A Reasonable Amount of Trouble
A Haunting at Marianwood

Short Stories:

Murder Under Sun
Anthology: *Derby Rotten Scoundrels*

If the Horseshoe Fits
Anthology: *Low Down and Derby*

The Long and Shorter of It
Anthology: *Mystery with a Splash of Bourbon*

A Haunting at Marianwood

Mystery and Horror, LLC
Clearwater, FL

A Haunting at Marianwood

Trade Paperback Edition
Sarah E. Glenn, Editor
Copyright © 2022 by Mystery and Horror, LLC
Published by Mystery and Horror, LLC

ISBN: 978-1-949281-23-1

CAST OF CHARACTERS

MARIANWOOD

Sister Miriam Patrice (Miri Pat): President of the Sisters of the Blessed Mother of God
Sister Annalise: Assistant to Sister Miriam Patrice

Sisters Agnes Marie, Edith, Bernadette, Joseph Thomas, Regina: Residents of the Motherhouse, elderly, retired

Mother Althea: Foundress of the order, deceased

Sister Euphoria: Deceased teacher at the school

Victoria Harris: Daughter of Matthias Harris, Gifted the land and house to the Sisters a hundred years ago; Deceased

Mr. Dowd: Manager of the buildings and grounds at Marianwood

Oliver (Ollie) Vincent: Farmworker at Marianwood

Delmar Boone: Resident at the retirement home; Uncle to Sister Annalise
Tatum (Tater) Boone: Nephew of Delmar and cousin to Sister Annalise

HAMMOND FAMILY AND FRIENDS

Dash (Dashiell) Hammond: Retired Army colonel, cousin to the McCaffertys, known problem solver

Mae (Maevis) Summers, M.D.: Wife of Dash, stepmother to T.J., childhood friend of the McCaffertys and Hammonds

T.J. (Thomas Joseph) Hammond: A curious confident four-year-old

Billy (William) McCafferty: Brother to Miri Pat and Dash's best friend; Attorney at Law

Owen (Grandpa) Hammond: Dash's father

Maria Hammond: Dash's sister-in-law

Irma and Ilene Tydie: Identical twins who are ex-nuns who work with Dash solving 'problems'

Grady Lennington: Retired Army Major; Dash's right-hand man during their military service; now head of Major Security, Inc.

Jumbo Washington and Tiny (Norman) Muldoon: Major Security operatives

DEDICATION:

For Lois, Mary Kay and Edie and all the Naz girls.
As always, for CJ the DJ, King of the Blues

THANKS:

Although not blessed with a biological sister, over the years I have formed bonds that are as close, if not closer, than a blood relative. This has to start with my kindergarten buddy, Laura Barda Thomas.

My Sisters in Crime chapter, Derby Rotten Scoundrels, all of them, has given me a revolving Rota of readers and writers to keep me almost honest and hard-working. They have infinite patience and overflowing optimism. The critique groups have, over the years, kept my nose to the grindstone.

And I would be remiss not to mention the ladies who read the first manuscript: Theresa Berry, Mary Kay Branton, Patience Martin and Lois Patrizia. Their kind words and questions made the book a better one.

The good Sisters at Nazareth changed my life for the better. A special thanks to Anna Marie Conklin and Barbara Peterson. May they rest in peace, the peace they never had while I was on campus.

Last, but never the least, is my daughter and best friend, Kristin.

Oops, how can I forget the contribution from my furry companions, Millie Jane and Daisy Rose, as well as Kristin's Charlie Cat. What they accidentally deleted while walking over the keyboard probably needed to go anyway.

CHAPTER ONE

Sister Miriam Patrice slid back from the kneeler. The quiet of the church soothed her as it wrapped its velvet cloak of serenity around her. She sat, hands folded, once in prayer but now to stop the trembling. Glancing at the sunlight streaming through the stained-glass windows casting a rainbow on the empty pews, she drew in deep slow breaths. She looked at the watch pinned to her tunic. Time to get back to work. She rose to leave the church, her place of refuge, a place free from the distractions of the running the community and the new retirement home the sisters established to help make ends meet.

The members of the Sisters of the Blessed Mother of God found their numbers dwindling. New recruits, as Sister Miriam Patrice called them mimicking her cousin Dash Hammond's military jargon, were very rare. The teaching congregation once had more than a hundred sisters. Vocations, callings to either the religious or the educational side of the community, had fallen to less than a handful each year.

As she walked down the aisle to the back of the church, she heard it again. Tap, tap, tap. She stopped to listen, making sure she wasn't mistaken. That sound sent shivers down her spine. Squaring her shoulders, she walked to the doors next to the church exit. One led up to the choir loft, the other down to the cellar. In days past she had gone up the stairs; today she would go down.

Pulling the doorknob, Miriam Patrice met the resistance

of a locked door. She pulled out her keys and unlocked it. She struggled with the door, suggesting to her that no one had gone to the cellar in a while.

The stone steps were worn but sturdy. She moved cautiously into the darkness, one hand on the wall to steady her nervous knees, the other searching for the handrail. Her hope was that the security guard forgot to close the door one day and some critter, not two legged, was trapped down here and making the tap, tap, tap sound. Logically she knew this was wrong, but the alternative could be worse.

Decades ago, they discovered one of the newer buildings constructed during a period of rapid expansion had been built on an underground spring. It wasn't long before the building tilted, as did their finances. What a waste of time and money. Fearful that what she would find was a tell-tale pooling or bubbling of water, she moved forward slowly. She said a silent prayer that she would not stumble into a puddle, a precursor of the inevitable unwelcome news.

Her trek seemed unnecessarily slow though reason told Miriam Patrice she should alert one of her sisters where she was just in case she lost her footing. But her reasoning had not been the sharpest of late. She blamed her sleepless nights, not because of an uneasy conscience but an overabundance of concern for her congregation and its uncertain future, both financially and individually.

After spending a half an hour poking into the corners, searching for the origin of the sound, Miriam Patrice gave up. She needed a flashlight if she wanted to do a proper search. Next time she would be prepared. Next time she told herself she would be less skittish, more confident that she could deal with whatever sprung up from the tap, tap, tap. After deciding this, she nodded to herself. At least she didn't hear a drip, drip, drip.

The sound had stopped so she decided to return to the church. As she locked the door behind her, the tap, tap, tap began again, louder this time. If she permitted herself, she would have said damn.

Stepping back into the body of the church, she brushed off her skirts, admonishing herself. She now had more laundry.

She walked outside into the cold January air. A smattering of snow still remained on the surfaces in shade. Fingering the key ring in her vast skirt pocket, she began the rounds of checking the numerous doors around the grounds. This had become her nightly routine for the last few weeks after the security guard had taken ill.

With that chore finished, she went into the dining hall to get a cup of hot tea. Her parents had been straight off the boat from Ireland and taught their children the value of a freshly brewed 'cuppa.'

As the sisters gathered for the evening meal, Miriam Patrice circulated among her good friends. She listened to their complaints of aching joints and joined in their lament about not being able to take a stroll around the grounds; it being so cold out. Reminding them that spring did come each year and would again, though not as quickly as they would like, she encouraged them to use this time for their indoor activities. There were quilts to be quilted for the summer festival and beads to be rolled so rosaries could be fashioned.

After her meal, complete with the warming tea, she walked the first-floor corridor, spending a few minutes with Sister Edith who was assigned to the desk in the foyer where visitors registered. Checking the book, she felt relieved. Everyone who had signed in had signed out.

"I'm going to lock the door. We should be visitor-free for the rest of the evening. If needed, remember the spare key is under the keyboard. If anyone knocks, be sure to see who it is before you let them in." Seeing the surprised look on Edith's face, Miriam Patrice felt a need to explain, but untruthfully. "The winter's darkness makes me jumpy. Feel like the wrong people are out after dark. Must be getting old," she laughed.

Sister Edith smiled, saying, "You getting old? Not

likely. You're a very spry 60-something; not like me, a very sedentary 80-something. Have a good evening. I'll call you if anyone knocks on the door. The outside lights are all on, right?"

Miriam Patrice nodded and moved onto her office to do some last-minute paperwork. There always seemed to be paperwork: small piles, large piles, never-ending piles. Finally, her eyes told her it was time to retire. Pocketing her glasses, she straightened the papers one last time. Now to get some rest so she would be ready to face a new day and decide what to do about the tap-tap-tap. She locked the door to her office, stopping to bid her assistant, Sister Annalise, who had the next office, a good night. She climbed the stairs to her room, opting not to take the elevator. She told herself she needed the exercise.

Her room, her second sanctuary. A comfortable bed, a bookcase containing her favorite titles and a nightstand where photos of her large family were featured. After changing into her nightgown, she reached under her pillow to retrieve the prayer book that once belonged to her mother. Not only were the prayers a comfort but to hold the book was like holding her mother's hand.

Nothing. No prayer book. Her heart jumped. She began to pull at the covers, patting them to locate the prayer book. On her knees, she searched under the bed. This wasn't possible. What the devil was going on? During this last month, a lot of her things were 'misplaced,' found where she was sure she hadn't left them.

She closed her eyes and said an all-too-familiar prayer to St. Anthony, patron saint of lost things. Squaring her shoulders, she began to search her room. And there it was, filed in the bookcase next to Agatha Christie's classic, *Murder in the Library.* She grasped the prayer book to her chest and moved to the rocking chair her brother Billy had given to her many years ago. An exact replica of the one their mother used to rock each of her ten babies. The most comfortable and comforting of chairs.

Taking several deep breaths, she felt a sense of peace. And determination. She locked the door, something she hadn't done in the ten years since she came back to the motherhouse. To think that someone had been in her room, violating her refuge, upset her. She told herself she wasn't crazy. But something had to be done. She perched on the side of the bed and looked at the phone on her nightstand. Taking another deep breath, she reached for it. Billy would know what to do. He may be her baby brother by ten years, but he was the smartest man she knew. And her aces in the hole were his two best friends, Dash Hammond and his wife, Dr. Maevis Summers.

She punched his icon. "Billy . . ."

Dash wandered into the kitchen where Mae sat with their son T.J. working on a page of the gigantic coloring book, a present from Santa. He smiled. Her auburn curls hid her green eyes. A sharp contrast to T.J.'s wavy black hair swept back from his face revealing big brown eyes, a gift from his birth mother. He leaned against the counter, knowing Mae would notice him and stop. He watched her turn, raise her eyebrows.

"Just got off the phone with good ole' Cousin Billy. Sister Miriam Patrice, she needs us. Just why is uncertain, other than something about weird things happening where she lives. Things that go bump in the night."

T.J. looked at his father. "Daddy, ghosts make noises that go bump in the night. Maybe it's ghosts. Or it could be goblins."

Dash sighed. "No T.J., no ghosts and no goblins." He looked at his wife who continued to color. "You know the motherhouse is in Kentucky." He shook his head. "Billy knows I said I'd never return to that state. One near-death experience is enough."

Mae tilted her head. "Chances of you being in another

near fatal auto accident have to be rather low, don't you think? Billy didn't define weird things by any chance, other than the bump in the night?"

"Details, details. All he said was that we were needed. Pretty sure she flashed the bat signal in the sky." He sighed a large sigh. "I told him no. No way."

"It is Miri Pat," Mae said. "She and her sisters prayed for you after the accident. Quite sure that's why you're alive."

"Remind me to send her a thank you card. No, Maevis, can't step into Kentucky. Not taking chances."

Dash poured himself a glass of milk. "I don't care if Mother Teresa or even my mother, God rest her soul, pleaded with me. No, a thousand times no." He downed the milk and rinsed the glass.

"It is Miri Pat," Mae said again.

His answer, "No, no."

He put the glass into the dishwasher. His fingers tap-tapped on the counter. He frowned, then grimaced. He watched his wife as she handed him the glasses from the table.

"What time are we leaving?" she asked.

Her husband scowled. "Zero six hundred, so get packing."

CHAPTER TWO

An early riser, Sister Annalise volunteered to do the first tour of the grounds. This was usually at six a.m., but today she was up extra early and on her way to the dining hall to make some coffee. Then she would unlock all those doors Miriam Patrice secured last night. Rather than walk outside, she chose to stay inside where it was considerably warmer.

As she rounded the corner on the first floor, she was surprised to see lights in the superior's office. She slowly pushed open the door to find Miriam Patrice in the office at this ungodly hour of four a.m.

"Miriam, what are you doing up so early? Didn't you think I would do my usual duty and unlock everything? I mean I've been doing it faithfully for quite a while now." She swept her hand toward Miriam Patrice's desk. "And what is with all the papers?"

Without looking up, Miriam Patrice replied, "Oh, Annalise, I'm sorry to have shocked you but I couldn't sleep. Last night I called my brother, Billy, William to you, asking if he could come down and review the plans I want to put before the board. You remember him from the board meetings. I just wanted a pair of fresh eyes. I didn't expect him to be able to come so quickly but he'll be here this afternoon. He's bringing our cousin, Dash. He's the soldier we prayed so hard for a few years back. Dash and his wife, Mae, and their little boy, are coming along for the ride." She stepped back from the stacks of papers on the table.

Annalise eyed Miriam Patrice with a suspicion. What was going on that Miriam called her brother? The semi-annual board meeting was in April, months away. Rather than ask those questions, she asked, "What can I do to help? Take a deep breath. Maybe we should make ourselves some tea or coffee if you don't want to go back to bed."

Miriam collapsed into a chair. "You're so right. Having a manic moment. Sure it will pass soon. Oh, the guest house. I'll need to make sure it's ready for them. Fresh sheets, towels, all the fixings. Need to get the heat going, make it comfortable." She sighed and started to push herself out of the chair.

Annalise stopped her. "Let me do that for you. After I do my rounds, I'll collect what's needed. Maybe, when Franny gets here, rather than clean in the motherhouse I'll take her with me, and we'll get the guest house shipshape. What time do you think they'll be here, surely not before six in the morning?"

"You're right. I should have most of the day though. If I'm right, Dash will have the troops up and out the door before daybreak. He always was an early riser like you."

Annalise frowned, searching her brain. "Oh, he's one of the kids from your old neighborhood. That's how you know about his sleeping habits. And his wife, is she the doctor you told me about? This will be an old family reunion for you." She pulled a chair over so she could sit next to Miriam. "I'll get the guest house ready, but only after the sun rises. Now I insist you return to your room. I'll walk with you. We both will need a few more hours before we entertain guests."

The two women walked together to the third floor where most of the sisters had rooms. Miriam's was the first on the left while Annalise's was on the other side and down three.

"Try to get some sleep. If you're not down by seven, I'll wake you. Agreed?" Annalise said.

"Agreed. And thanks for your offer of help. If you could get the guest house ready, that would be wonderful. Pleasant dreams, short that they may be." With that Miriam closed her door, silently turning the key.

Annalise continued to her room. She sat on her bed and pondered the arrival of William McCafferty, the brother. She knew him from the board meetings. One sharp dude as her younger self might have said. And now an unknown, this cousin/soldier and family. Why are all of them coming down in the middle, well, start of winter, to visit?

She checked the time. Too early to call her cousin. He'd be furious if she woke him at this hour. Rummaging around in her desk, she pulled out a handful of silver discs and put them in her pocket. Just what she needed for the guest house. Then she stretched out on her bed to get a bit more sleep. This weekend could be a very busy one and she needed her wits about her.

CHAPTER THREE

The Hammond trio was indeed up at dawn's early light. The car was packed with more provisions than Dash thought necessary until Mae reminded him of traveling with a four-year-old. She brought not only clothes but toys and books to entertain him on the drive and once there. All sorts of snacks, plus bottles of water for the big guys, added to the supplies.

Dash texted Billy when they left Clover Pointe to pick him up in Columbus. Two hours there and then another four hours to the convent, situated in central Kentucky, forty or so miles south of Louisville.

Glancing into the mirror so he could see Mae and T.J. in the back seat, he knew why the ride was so quiet. Heads leaning together, both were sound asleep.

The stop at Billy's house lasted longer than Dash wanted, but no way could they not talk to Elena, Billy's wife. And time for a quick potty break for the little one and his mother. In true military fashion, Dash declared there would be no breaks for lunch and only one short pee stop.

While Mae and T.J. quietly read books in the back, Dash asked Billy, "Any more thoughts on why we, or more specifically you, were summoned? Hate to say, but I don't remember the last time I saw Miri Pat." He held up his hand. "Yes, I know she came to see me in the hospital but, as you recall, I didn't recognize myself much less the rest of you do-gooders."

Billy laughed. "Ah, those were the days. You were at our mercy. You're just lucky to have such good kind relatives who didn't drop you off in Yuma or some such place to fend on your own."

Dash rolled his eyes. "Yes, every night I thank the good Lord for his foresight in giving me such wonderful people at a time of crisis in my life. Now, dear cuz, back to the matter at hand. You are on the board for the community or congregation, right? What are they up to that we need to appear in the harsh midwinter?"

"Technically, I think we're still in the harsh beginning of winter ..."

Exasperated Dash said, "Whatever! Any idea what we face?"

"No, and that's what has me worried enough to ask you along. I know full well how you feel about crossing the Ohio River into Kentucky, but you know full well that the chances of another accident are slim and none. Having said all that, you also know that Miri Pat is one of the most competent women on this earth. They trusted her with guiding them through some rough waters. She had the good sense to form a lay board to give advice. Along with me, she brought our little brother Tommy as the accountant as well as a businesswoman from Bardstown, a priest, and a minister. She's hoping betwixt and between all of us we might have one or two good suggestions to keep the congregation afloat."

Dash glanced at his cousin who was chewing on his thumb nail. "Don't worry. Once there, we'll get some answers and soon have all this sorted. Weekend at the most. Trust me. Even if ghosts are involved, they won't stand a chance against this big bad ex-soldier."

Mae took this opportunity to snicker loudly. T.J. sat wide-eyed at the mention of ghosts. He then burst into song, 'who you gonna call?'

It was early afternoon when the car turned off the highway and rounded the lane heading to the motherhouse, officially known as Marianwood. The road took them past a small lake, complete with a walking path and benches. It was only a few minutes before they came upon the graveyard. Rows of white headstones. One huge mausoleum in the middle. A chill ran down Dash's spine. He stopped abruptly and got out of the car to stare at the cemetery.

Standing with correct military posture as his eyes moved from row to row, he breathed slowly as his mind substituted another cemetery before him. Arlington. Taps. Peterson. Taps. Beaumont. He closed his eyes before the tears threatening to overflow started.

A slight pressure on his hand. Mae. A touch was all he needed. Message received. A quick swipe across his face and they walked slowly to the car.

He sat down and glanced at Billy who nodded quietly, acknowledging that he understood. "Not exactly tourist brochure material. First thing you see is a cemetery. Might be good for new recruits, everlasting home and all." Dash shivered. "Am I the only one who gets the feeling there's no way outta here? No wonder Miri Pat hears voices. She's lucky that's all that is coming from over there."

"Daddy, are the ghosts talking? Do you think we'll hear them?"

Dash murmured, "That's all we need. All I need."

They drove past the security hut across from the cemetery and turned onto the road leading to the motherhouse, church and other buildings.

Suddenly there she was. Miri Pat. Standing in front of a house across from the church, she waved madly, jumping up and down. Dash pulled the car to the curb thinking of the uncharacteristic behavior of his religious cousin. He watched her run to the passenger door and yank it open, pulling at her brother before he could unhook the seat belt. She wrapped her arms around him, crying into his coat.

He turned to Mae. "A little over-enthusiastic, don't you

think? Hell, it's just her brother. Very un-nun-like. Not happy, Maevis my love. Something rotten is going on here." He exited the car, opening the door for Mae and helping T.J. out of the car seat. He listened patiently as his son grumbled about being stiff from sitting so long.

Dash moved his family onto the sidewalk where Miri Pat still clung to her brother. He pried her from Billy's arms.

"Happy New Year, Miri Pat, no tears now. Billy is hardly worth this display of familial love. Now let me introduce to someone worthy of tears. T.J., front and center." He squatted down to look his son directly in the eyes. "T.J., this is another of Billy's sisters. Sister Miriam Patrice lives down here, which is why you haven't met her until now. So, please shake her hand, or better yet, give Miri Pat a kiss."

T.J. flashed a big smile and extended his hand. "Why are you crying? Are you hurt? Mommy's a doctor and she can take care of you." He stopped momentarily to take a breath and then continued, "Why are you a sister and not an auntie like Peggy? She's Uncle Billy's sister, too. He has a lot of them, and I don't have any." He added this with an eye roll.

Sister Miriam Patrice shook his hand and stooped down. She reached out to touch the toddler's face. "Yes, I guess I'm an honorary auntie of sorts like Peggy. And you, you curly headed sweetheart, are a chip off the old block. I bet you're a handful just like your dear old dad."

"Why do you wear that long dress and funny hat? Are you going to a party?" Thomas asked.

"No, this is my habit, my uniform. See I'm a soldier in Christ's army."

T.J. responded, "My mama was a soldier, but she got sick and has to live with Jesus now." He pointed to his father. "He was a soldier too so he can save you from your ghosts or goblins."

Miri Pat stood to look at her brother. "Ghosts. Goblins?"

Billy just shrugged and looked heavenward.

Dash stepped forward. "I'd love to know the answer to that. I've had to listen to the Ghostbuster song all the way down here. Please, Miri, find one ghost for us that will scare the pants off T.J. and quiet him down."

Sister touched the right side of his face, shaking her head. "You look so much better than when I saw you in the hospital, what is it now, six years ago. Thought you were a goner. Said a few prayers for you."

"So I understand. Thank you and all your good sisters. Mae says that's the reason I'm alive."

"No, no. The reason you're alive is that God has his hands full and doesn't want you up there fussing around with everything. He's going to let you mess with we mortals for many more years before He opens the celestial gates to you."

Mae stepped forward to give her old friend a hug. "Miri, it's wonderful to see you. Sorry you're having some trouble down here, but you asked the right people for help. How about we move inside and out of the chill? Are we getting right down to business, or can we catch up a bit?"

"Billy texted that you didn't stop for lunch, so I took the liberty of ordering some fried chicken and fixings for you. Wouldn't be Kentucky if we didn't chow down on our favorite dish." She turned to Dash. "It's not the colonel's chicken, Colonel. It's our special recipe which I think is better." She took T.J.'s hand, asking him, "You do like fried chicken, don't you?"

T.J.'s eyes lit up. A big smile broke out on his face. "Yes, ma'am. And mashed potatoes and corn on the cob."

"Okay troops, forward march." Dash said, then looked at Miri Pat. "Oops, as soon as you tell us which way is forward."

Sister Miriam Patrice pointed to the house behind them. She explained, "This was the former rectory. During our heyday, there was a full staff of professors and priests to educate the novices and local young women who chose not to travel to the big city for college. The men lived here.

"You can park in front. Don't know how much luggage you have but this spot will be easier to unload. We don't really have a garage or carport close but if you want, I'll show you where they are after we eat."

Dash and Billy grabbed the bags, backpacks, toys, and books. They looked at each other, a silent message about how much stuff could one child need.

As they entered the house, Miri Pat said, "There are two bedrooms upstairs; each has a double bed. I brought a cot over for Thomas. Separate baths, and voila," She pointed to the small kitchen area where the table was piled high with platters of chicken and several side dishes.

The aroma reminded the travelers they were hungry, or "starving" as T.J. put it. He rushed to the table, pulling out a chair and climbing on it. As he reached to grab the chicken, his father stepped in to carry him to the sink for the cleansing of the hands. After washing up themselves, Mae and Miri gathered plates and utensils. After a prayer of thanksgiving for the food and safe arrival, Miri passed out the nourishment.

As they were eating, Miri Pat asked the littlest person at the table. "Do you prefer Thomas or T.J.?"

Billy snorted and pointed to the pile of bones on T.J.'s plate. "Just don't call him late for fried chicken."

"Quiet, William, I want to ask Thomas about the ghosts and goblins. Please tell me about them, and why do you think we have some here?"

T.J. began, "Well, Sister, Daddy said Uncle Billy said you heard strange noises and things went bump in the night. Ghosts sometimes make noises, but they usually are friendly and just want to talk to you."

Billy interrupted, "Are they all called 'Casper' as in the friendly ghost?"

Frowning at his honorary uncle, T.J. continued, "Now, a goblin is a nasty thing. He likes to play pranks and moves things around. If you have to have one or the other, take a ghost."

Miri Pat smiled, "And how do you know all this?"

"Well, Stevie Parker is a boy in my class at school and his older brother Ned has been reading up on ghosts and goblins. He's an expert now. He told Stevie and Stevie told me."

"And how old is this Ned Parker, if I might inquire?" Dash asked.

T.J.'s brow wrinkled as he thought. "I think he might be in the second grade but maybe the third. He's kinda old."

It was Billy's turn to jump in. "Oh, that Ned Parker. Of course, silly Billy, that's me."

Changing the subject, T.J. pulled a stuffed raggedy rabbit out of his backpack. He introduced Petey to Miri Pat explaining how the toy came with him from Philly when he had to move in with Dash.

They all pushed back from the table, full of chicken and good cheer.

A big sigh escaped from Billy. "Okay, sis, spill. If I may be so crass, what the hell is going on? This isn't some hormonal crisis, is it?"

"Ah, the diplomat speaks." Dash laughed. "Sorry, I'm usually the one with my foot in my mouth. Right now, it's too full of chicken." He handed Billy another piece. "Here gnaw on this."

Miri Pat looked around the table. "William, I wish I knew what was going on, but I don't. I'm hearing noises that don't make any sense and I even hear mumbling voices. I put something in one place and then it appears in another. For all I know I'm losing it. Didn't think that ran in the family but there's a first time for everything."

"Where are you when you hear these noises? The voices, can you understand what is being said?" Dash asked.

"In the church there's a tap, tap, almost like dripping water but can't find any source. Now I will admit to not climbing up onto the roof, but I did try to explore the cellar. The voices I hear in a variety of places. My room, my office, the chapel. And, no, mumbled words, some singing, but nothing I can really understand."

Billy jumped in to ask. "Anyone else hearing these noises, voices?"

His sister blushed. "I've been afraid to ask, for fear they'll think I'm crazy. But no one has reported anything to me." She leaned back in her chair, shaking her head. "What do you think? Have I dragged you down here on a fool's errand?"

Mae reached across the table to take Miri's hand. "These fools need an errand, so don't worry about that." She stood to gather the dishes. "Gentlemen, what's your next step?"

Billy spoke up. "Miri, did you get the information I requested?"

Sister pointed to the front room where a stack of papers lay on the coffee table, next to rolls of architectural plans. "In there. Gathered what I could on such short notice." She reached into the deep pocket of her habit, pulling out a single sheet of paper. "I've listed as best as I can remember what, when and where. The beginning is sparse as I didn't realize I'd need the dates, etc."

Dash took the paper and reviewed it. "No one ever knows exactly when these things start, as we don't expect to be in the middle of anything until we are up to our eyebrows. This is good." He turned to his comrades. "Ready to walk off the chicken. How about an in-depth tour of the premises? It'll be getting dark soon and I'd like to get my bearings before the sun goes down. Then I'll take everyone into town for some dessert."

T.J. jumped up. "Ice cream! Sister Miri, do you like ice cream?"

"I sure do but there's no need to go into town. We have a marvelous ice cream machine in our dining area. How about we wind up our tour there? Okay with you, Master Hammond?" Sister asked.

Nodding vigorously, T.J. smiled. "A whole ice cream machine. Daddy, can we get one?" When no one moved, the child commanded, "Let's get started."

They gathered their coats, gloves and hats. The January air had more of a bite to it now that there was a slight breeze, cutting right through their outer garments. A light coating of snow covered the grass but not the sidewalks and roads.

If Sister Miriam Patrice needed a job other than president, she could be a first-class tour guide. She not only gave historical information but architectural as well.

When they reached the far end of the buildings, Miri Pat swept her hand across the vista. "When I entered the congregation over forty years ago, all that was grazing pasture. There was a dairy farm and even a small herd of cattle here. Through the years those ventures were dismantled one by one. Now we grow flowers and herbs." She pointed again. "Over there we have a large vegetable garden. We're trying to become self-sufficient. And somewhere out back there is a building that houses laying chickens. Any surplus we sell, just like the old farm wives did for years. A few pennies here and there."

Dash mouthed "pennies" to Billy who shrugged.

The tour continued. Per Dash's instructions, Miri Pat pointed out each and every door and lock. She handed him the key ring. There were at least fifteen keys, some that Miri Pat had no idea what they opened.

"How many people have copies of all these keys?" he asked.

She shrugged. "Let's see. I have a set of exterior and a set of the interior ones. My assistant, Sister Annalise, does the morning unlocking so she has both sets as well. We rarely lock the interior doors to the offices, chapel and work areas such as laundry. The security men definitely have the exterior set as part of their job is to walk the grounds making sure we're all locked in. The director and assistant of the retirement quarters would have a set for their building, but not the motherhouse. Mr. Dowd, our facilities manager, has a partial set. One or two of his men might have particular keys, say to the barn which houses the tractors, mowers and such. Honestly, there might be others, but I'm sorry I don't have a listing."

Billy said, "That security service, you mentioned, any reports from them about suspicious activity?"

"No. Well, in all fairness, I should say that they haven't been on the job for several weeks now. It's a small two-man firm. John is currently on vacation, visiting his daughter in sunny Florida. His brother Borland has been in the hospital since right before Christmas, going on three weeks now. We've been without the nightly checks, except for what I do."

"And all these noises, voices started when?" Dash pulled out the sheet she had given him.

Billy answered for her. "Don't bother. Let me guess. This nonsense started when the guards left their post. Sis, wanna bet there is a correlation?"

Mae stepped between the siblings. "Miri don't let him intimidate you. Remind him that you changed his diapers. Always shuts them up."

"So a lot of keys floating around. Why so many different locks? No one ever thought to streamline all this?" Dash asked, wondering aloud at this inefficiency.

The tour lasted a good hour and change. Dash checked every door and suggested half the locks be upgraded to more secure ones. He recorded all this in his ever-present notebook. Since he would do the first patrol after dark, he needed to know which keys opened which doors.

Mae stepped forward. "Can we see a bit of the inside? It's bound to be warmer there. I know I'm a bit of wuss, but my toes have lost all feeling. And Thomas is wearing out, not to mention freezing. And he is being so patient about the promise of ice cream."

Dash looked over to his son who was jiggling up and down trying to keep warm. He picked up his son. "Sister, if you please."

They entered through O'Bryan Hall, where the reception area was located. Miri Pat introduced them to Sister Edith. She was the main receptionist. Wheelchair-bound, she covered most of the hours at this front desk. She explained the sign-in procedure. "We instituted this about four years ago when we realized we had a lot of visitors wandering where they shouldn't. If nothing else we now know we should be looking for someone if not everyone has signed out at closing time, which is seven during the winter hours and nine starting in April and running until end of September."

Billy touched his sister's arm. "The security system I recommended. Has it been installed yet?"

Miri Pat shrugged. "It's on the 'to do' list, moving slowly up to the top. I guess I should fast-track it."

After glancing quickly into a few of the darkened rooms on the main floor, they adjourned to the dining hall located on the lowest level. Many of sisters were still enjoying their Saturday evening meal which consisted of sandwiches and dessert—T.J.'s favorite. After a quick walkabout to introduce her guests, Miri Pat settled them at a table.

After getting the promised ice cream cone for his son, Dash leaned over to Miri Pat. "How'd we get fried chicken while your lot are eating sandwiches? Why do I get the feeling God is going to slap my hand for that?"

Laughing, she said, "Well, my lot, as you call my sisters, are very used to this Saturday meal. Also gives our cooks some time off. Sunday is the same, though often leftovers from Saturday and Sunday lunches can be found. Our main meal is after Mass which ends around eleven thirty. Evening meals are light fare, better for folks our age. But since you're my guests and I just knew two strapping men and one growing child needed more than cold cuts to see them through the night, I ordered the fried chicken for you."

"You're a real gem, Miri Pat, always were. You did an excellent job of raising us kids and now you're taking care of a whole new flock. What is it the sisters used to say when we were in school---something about a higher place in heaven? You'll be at the top." Dash smiled.

He watched as one of the sisters waved to Miri Pat motioning her to join her table.

Sister Miriam Patrice took T.J. by the hand. "I want you to meet Sister Agnes Marie. She is our resident expert on ghosts. She'll know if any ghosts are roaming our house and grounds."

Dash followed them so he would know where to look for these otherworldly beings.

CHAPTER FOUR

Sister Agnes Marie had coke-bottle glasses and skin that looked as soft as cotton. Her face was one big wrinkle, but her clear blue eyes twinkled when asked about the ghosts. She held out her hands inviting T.J. to sit with her. Instead, he shyly climbed onto Sister Miriam Patrice's lap and settled in to hear the stories.

"Well, little one, there are rumors of several different ghosts that make their home with us and appear at random, at least to us, times. One lives right here in this building. If you walk down the hall from the drawing room, you will find a spiral staircase leading to the floors above. The curve is very tight so some of the steps are very narrow, and you have to be careful. Unfortunately, this was the easiest route for our novices, those are young women who just joined the congregation, to reach their rooms. Sister Euphonia was a stern taskmaster and not necessarily a favorite with her charges."

Dash pulled up a chair sensing this was going to be an amusing story.

Agnes Marie studied T.J.'s face, his eyes growing large in anticipation.

"Now one thing Sister Euphonia hated was tardiness. Do you know what that is?"

T.J. nodded. "That's when you didn't finish your chores on time, and everyone has to wait for you."

"Yes, that's when you are late for your class or appointment. Woe betide if any of the girls were late.

Euphonia tucked herself into a corner at the top of the stairs and stepped out when the girl ran up the stairs. Once the young girl was so frightened, she fell backwards down the stairs, breaking her arm and leg."

"Yikes," T.J. said, waiting for more.

"Well, years later, Sister Euphonia was found at the base of the staircase, dead with her neck broken. All sorts of rumors flew; was it an accident or was she pushed?"

T.J.'s eyes opened wider. He turned to Sister Miriam Patrice. "You're not supposed to push people on the stairs. Mommy says that's not very nice, and Daddy says it's dangerous."

His focus returned to Sister Agnes Marie. "Have you ever seen her? The ghost on the staircase I mean."

Sister shook her head. "No, but I've talked with others who swear they have. Now, do you have time for one more quick story? This one has to do with the specter, that's another word for ghost, in the graveyard."

Dash interrupted. "I can see where a ghost might want to haunt that cemetery. Gave me the willies just driving by."

He blushed when Agnes Marie looked sternly at him, silently asking if he was finished. Feeling transported back to his grade school days, he nodded sheepishly.

She continued, "Many, many years ago before this was our motherhouse, it was a plantation." When she saw the quizzical look on the boy's face, she explained. "A plantation is a very big farm with a big house. In fact, we're sitting in an updated, expanded version of that house."

T. J. nodded as if he understood.

Sister carried on. "Victoria, daughter of Matthias Harris, fell in love with a poor farmer who lived in the town. Her father forbade the marriage and there were many screaming matches between father and daughter. Victoria decided to elope." Again, Sister stopped to clarify. "That means she was going to run away from home. She packed a small bag and snuck out of the house to walk into town where she would meet her beau. As she crossed what is now the graveyard, she ran into her father. He stopped her, saying the young man was dead and now buried somewhere in that large plot of land."

With a sigh, Sister continued, "He dragged her back to the house where many years later she died of a broken heart, but not before spending all of her time searching for his grave."

Sister lowered her voice, "Now when there's a full moon, you might catch a glimpse of her searching. You'll recognize her as she wears a long flowing dress and a wide-brimmed hat." She winked at T.J. who shivered.

Dash leaned in. "Ah, full moon. Getting close to one so she could be searching tonight. In other words, if I see a young woman in the graveyard, it's Victoria. Right?"

Sister Agnes Marie smiled, nodding gently. "She won't hurt you but might ask if you know where her beau is buried." She started to rise. "Now gentlemen, I'm off to watch my British comedies. Seen them a million times but they always make me laugh. Let me know if you encounter either of these ghosts. And to be sure, I have more to share with you tomorrow."

T.J. frowned. "Someone needs to tell Victoria to look in the lake. Maybe her father threw the body there. That's what daddy does after he shoots someone."

That stopped Sister Agnes Marie. All the sisters at the table stared at the assassin daddy.

Dash's head dropped to his chest when he saw the shocked faces.

Sister Miriam Patrice's shoulders shook with laughter. "Something you want to share with us, Dash?"

He glared at his son. "Yes, the next body into the lake won't make much of a splash." He looked into their faces. Raising his right hand, he said, "You do know he is just talking nonsense. Haven't tossed any bodies into any lake, I swear."

Grabbing his son's hand, he said, "Say goodnight, T.J."

26

CHAPTER FIVE

T. J. bounced back to his mother so he could share the stories while Dash backed away, pleading his innocence with each step. Miri Pat followed, laughing and shaking her head.

When back at their table, Dash looked to Miri Pat who just raised her eyebrows.

"You did say you wanted a ghost and Agnes Marie gave you two."

"You put any credence in these stories?"

"About as much as what T.J. said about you. Let's say I've heard of close encounters from other sisters and visitors so I'm keeping an open mind."

Miri reached across the table to tap Dash's hand. "Walk with me for a bit. I'd like a chat."

Dash looked at his wife and then Billy. When neither offered to come along, he stood motioning for Miri Pat to lead the way.

She tucked his arm in hers and led him into the hallway and up the stairs to the main floor.

"I haven't seen you since the accident and, being the old nosey neighbor, I have some questions for you, ones I'm sure you would answer differently if Mae and Billy were present."

Dash looked at her suspiciously. He licked his lips and tilted his head thinking this can't be good.

Miri smiled, "You were always my favorite, but don't

tell Billy or Mae."

"Ah, Miri, please. That would ruin their day and make mine."

The sister just continued, "You are one of my dearest people. Such a rascal as a child and I can say that you've grown into a fine man."

Dash chuckled, "Lordy, Miri Pat, you're going to have me blushing in a minute. Fine man, indeed. Could I get you to have a talk with Owen? My father might be coming round to me being a decent person, but fine man might be pushing his limits."

Miri stopped to face him, still holding his arm. "Nonsense. He might say one thing to your face but behind your back he is in awe of you."

Now it was Dash's turn to pull away. "And just what are you smoking, and can I have some? When did he say something like that if I may ask?"

She continued to walk. "When we talked in the hospital after your accident, your father was very emotional, worried that he missed so much with you and really worried he'd never have the chance."

"Don't suppose you recorded this exchange because I'd like a copy."

"No, silly, I didn't. At the time we all, and that includes those doctors at the hospital, were sure you wouldn't make it." She shook her head, closing her eyes. "I can still see you. All bandages and tubes. I was only in the room for a minute but can't get those beep-beep sounds out of my head, not when I think of you."

Dash stopped again. Before he answered he pursed his lips together and frowned as he searched for the right answer. "Between your prayers and my never-ending duty to prove everyone wrong, I guess I survived out of sheer bullheadedness." He smiled mischievously. "Want to know a secret?"

She nodded.

"I wasn't unconscious; I could hear all of you moaning and groaning about how you should have treated me better. I just played along since it seemed a shame to let everyone down by dying."

Miri smirked. "Yeah, right. So now, tell me how civilian life is treating you? I want the truth. I could always tell when you were fibbing."

"Okay, if you really want to know, my dear almost mother, as for the forced civilian life, the first two years were spent trying to recover so I'd rate them middling to fair. You know faking it so the family would feel like they were doing charitable deeds. The next several years I spent doing my fair share of carousing and more than my fair share of drinking so perfect for this soldier but not so good for his father and the rest of the family. So I settled down a bit. I've been a substitute teacher and coach; did a lot of renovation work on the old homestead. And I work with the vets in town and around the country. All that was more out of self-interest than helping others." He took a deep breath. "And then along came T.J. Talk about life-changing event."

He moved to lean his back against the wall, hands tucked behind him. "Don't know if I can express how I felt when I got the call. Stupefied might be the word, but then when I actually knelt in front of that little, brown-eyed wisp of a boy, I thought my heart would explode. To say that I had given up on having children would not be an understatement."

Miri Pat looked at him. "I bet there were many women out there who would have loved to have you father their children. For example, the woman who gave you T.J. Adoption, did you and Mae never consider that? I understand how rough it was after your baby died, but what happened?"

Dash shook his head and glanced at his watch. "We don't have enough time to go into all of that. Another woman, heresy. In my mind, it was always Mae for me since we were kids. And after our little babe died, the words, the hours, the tears on both our parts would fill a library of books of how to, how not to, what to say, what not to say.

I was just happy I had a son. Boys I can understand. Women, little girls, no idea, especially if they have red hair."

Laughing, Miri said, "Pretty sure Mae would say 'auburn' not red."

Dash snorted. "Ha, listen, I've seen her top to toe over a lifetime and I can state that the auburn is from a bottle and not God."

"Oh, so you're going down there, are you?"

"As often as she will let me," he said with a wink. He faced his cousin, looking directly into her eyes.

"Now that I've revealed my soul to you, and you were right, I might not have said some of that with Mae present. It's your turn. What the hell is going on and why was it important that Mae and I came along?"

Wrinkling her nose, she smiled. "You always were the clever one, the suspicious one. William is a very capable man, but he's led a quiet life even if he spends his time defending criminals. The three of you together are a formidable team and that was what I needed. Whatever is going on, and something is, I'm not crazy, senile or hallucinating. I don't have enough expertise in the ways of the world. If someone is harassing me, I want to know why. I mean, what can I be doing that is so upsetting someone can't just come to me and say 'Miriam Patrice, you're doing this all wrong'."

Dash leaned into Miri, "Just what are you doing? Or should I say what is it you do?"

"I have been assigned to protecting the community, spiritually, financially, and practically. There is a goodly amount of money involved but the lay board has helped with securing the funds, investing the funds. There is even a group of retired sisters who have taken courses on investing and now study the market to make recommendations, etc. So it's not just me signing checks, throwing money out the window or hoarding it in my closet." She shrugged. "I just don't understand all this. Sure, I've had my head in the clouds too long. When I was a school principal, I was more attuned to pranks and jokes, if that's what all this is."

They returned to the dining room and chatted as the sun went down. Now warm, with full bellies, the yawns began. When Miri Pat reached out to her brother, she said, "Thank you for coming. Just having you here makes me feel so much better."

Dash stood. "I'm thinking you just need a good night's sleep. Here's what we'll do. You sleep at the guest house with Mae, and I'll sleep in your room tonight. I can listen for voices, record what I hear. I'll prowl around a bit to see what's going on. Then we can determine just how nuts you are or are not."

He watched as Billy glanced at Mae who looked at Miri who sat with her mouth open.

Clearing his throat, Billy said, "Dash, pretty sure we know who the nut is. Did you listen to what you just suggested? That you sleep in Miri's room. And just where would that room be, I ask politely?"

"Oh." Dash nodded slowly, biting his lip. "Right. Got it. Not the best idea for me to sleep here. Sorta negates the separation of sexes."

Mae started laughing. "Just what these poor women need. You, the manly man, prowling around in his PJ's, weapon in hand, listening at doors. Almost wish we could film it for this year's stupid family photos."

T.J. tugged at Miri's sleeve. "Why are you laughing at my dad?"

"Because he said something silly, that's all. We'll keep him from doing something silly." Miri answered. "Dash, I have to ask, do you have a gun? Because we don't allow them here. Don't know where you'll keep it but..."

Dash raised his hand to stop her. "Non-negotiable my friend. Once I know who or what we're facing, then we can talk about going about unarmed." He patted his back where his weapon lodged in his belt. "Until then."

"Not happy, Dashiell."

"No one ever is. Now you get some sleep. I do believe I have just the solution to in-house undercover agents."

Mae sat up straight. "Not me, please. My mother, a good Irish mother, wanted me to be a nun. Sadly, didn't take with me. Everyone knew some young blue-eyed lad had 'despoiled' me. Ruined forever."

Dash frowned then shook his head. Holding up two fingers, he put his hand out to indicate 'about this tall.'

"Excellent. How are you going to get them down here? That rickety car of theirs will never make it. Oh, I know, tell them to take my car. They can get the keys from your dad or brother and drive on down. Two birds with one stone: they have a safe ride down and I'll have my wheels to head home if you and Billy decide to make a week of this."

Dash turned to Miri Pat. "We have two very wonderful friends who happen to be twins and ex-sisters. They've helped me on several other projects. Still have their habits and could pose as prospective transfers to your congregation."

"May I ask why they left the convent?" Miri Pat asked cautiously, not sure she wanted to hear the answer.

"Not so much left as booted out. Something to do with a gun, bad parish and their superior's interpretation of non-violence even in protection of themselves," Mae explained.

Billy reached over to his sister. "Trust us on this. They are delightful, perfect undercover agents. Irma is an ex-teacher, principal. A parishioner taught her how to handle a gun since the neighborhood where the sisters taught and lived was riddled with crime and trouble was getting rather close to them. Ilene is a nurse. The twins refused to be separated, so when Irma was booted out, Ilene waved goodbye."

T.J. raised his hand. "They are excellent babysitters too. Irma is teaching me to write."

Defeated, Miri Pat scowled. "Good references, huh? I look forward to meeting them. Now I think I will bid you all goodnight and turn in early. Perchance to sleep."

Billy kissed his sister's cheek and reminded her to lock her door. T.J. and Mae also doled out goodnight kisses.

Dash commandeered Sister's set of exterior keys. "I'm going to make a round or two later. Familiarize myself with the grounds."

"Will you remember all that we saw, talked about?"

"Never fear, this is second nature to me. Get some rest. The cavalry, or at least one member of it, has arrived." Dash said with a wink and a nod.

CHAPTER SIX

Dash waited in the hall while his troops visited the bathrooms before the short trip to the guest house. He studied the portrait of a very stern woman. Frowning, he strained to read her name: Mother Althea.

Sister Agnes Marie hurried toward him waving a pamphlet. "Ah, Colonel, I was hoping to catch you. Wanted to give you this. It's my humble gift to the community, a history of them and this land."

She pointed to the portrait. "That's Mother Althea, the foundress. She was the one who negotiated with Miss Victoria for a portion of the land to build the motherhouse. To her amazement, Miss Victoria invited the small band of women to live with her in the interim. In the end, Miss Victoria gave Mother Althea the whole plantation with the caveat she could live out her years here. Built a Reading Room as her sanctuary, private space until she died. It's a delightful room right around the corner. Be sure to visit it."

Taking the pamphlet, Dash said, "Thanks. Sounds like a very interesting history. And this is a beautiful place. You're a lucky woman, all this beauty and a ghost or two."

Mae, T.J. and Billy who were ready to head to the guest house joined them, beginning the round of good nights. As they exited the motherhouse, T.J. raised his hand. "Mommy, can we go for a walk? Maybe we'll see the ghosts."

Dash nodded. "Excellent idea, kiddo. Give me a chance

for a second look. Let's stroll down to the security station. We'll get their perspective on what they can/cannot see."

Pulling their hats down over their ears and tucking scarves tightly around their necks, they walked down the road behind the guest house and in the front of the cemetery. They poked around the little hut with the big security sign but found nothing.

As they began the walk back, Mae stopped, jerking Dash's hand. "Look, over there, in the cemetery."

The quartet stopped. Dash hoisted T.J. up on his shoulders so the little one could see. They stood quietly and watched as a vision of a woman walked slowly around the far end of the cemetery. She wore a long filmy dress and a big-brimmed hat. She stopped and tapped the ground ever so often.

"Miss Victoria! Daddy, do you see her? Do you think it's her?" T.J. whispered.

Smiling, Dash said, "Yes, ever so convenient too. Well, let's stroll along and see if we can help Miss Victoria look for her lover's grave."

Mae took hold of Billy and Dash, so the trio of adults marched quietly toward the specter. T.J. squirmed on his father's shoulders causing Dash to remind his son to sit still so he didn't fall off.

Once they were fairly close to the opening to the cemetery, Dash swung T.J. down handing him to Mae. Starting off with a slow jog, the ex-soldier headed toward the far end where the vision in white walked slowly. As he picked up the pace, he watched her turn toward him, stop and then start running among the tombstones finally stepping behind the large family crypt.

When Dash stepped off the road, Billy called after him. "Be careful. Graveyards are notoriously uneven. Can't have you breaking an arm or a leg."

Billy, Mae and T.J. raced to catch up to Dash, but he waved them back. He pointed to the snow-covered ground.

"Stop. Footprints. I'm tracking them." He pulled out his phone and snapped a variety of shots. He disappeared behind the large monument, then looked back at Billy "Damn! The footprints stop. Where the hell did she go?" He started prodding and pushing at the marble tombstone. When nothing moved, he walked back to the road.

"Damnedest thing. The footprints are all over the path she was on but when she went around the tombstone, they stopped. Helluva trick. Sister Agnes Marie set us up properly. Wonder how they did that and who they got to wander around on this frosty night."

"Daddy, it was the ghost of Miss Victoria." T.J.'s brow wrinkled in thought. "But ghosts don't leave footprints, do they, Uncle Billy?"

"Kid's got a point. Let's head back to the house. I've got chills all over and not necessarily from the cold. Bet we can find some hot chocolate to make. Race you to the house." And Billy sprinted off. T.J. broke free from his mother and gave chase.

Mae waited for Dash. "You think this is a hoax? Really? Why would the sisters do that to us?"

"A non-threatening ghost. Who knows?" He guided Mae toward the house. "No matter what, hot chocolate does sound delicious."

With Sister Agnes Marie's pamphlet in hand, Dash climbed into bed. T.J. curled up with Petey Rabbit on the cot. Mae sat reading an old paperback.

"Whatcha reading?" Dash asked.

"*A League of Frightened Men*, an Archie Goodwin book. Can't get enough of Archie. You should be more like him, you know," Mae said.

"Pretty sure that's a Nero Wolfe book. And, my dear lady, what does good old Archie have or do that I don't?"

Mae thought about her answer. "Not sure. Just know you're lacking something. I'll get back to you on that."

"I'm sure you will." Dash opened the pamphlet and began reading.

After a few minutes, he felt a nudge from his bedmate.

"Whatcha reading?"

"Sister Agnes Marie has thoughtfully provided a brief history of the community which contains an even shorter history of Victoria Harris. I'm doing my research on our friendly ghost. Can't be too prepared nowadays. And I definitely can't have Ned Parker, the grade school expert on ghosts, knowing more than I do."

Mae leaned over to read the pamphlet along with her husband.

He bookmarked his spot and closed the booklet. Putting his free arm around Mae, he pulled her closer.

"Now I will admit to not knowing everything there is to know about everything or even anything, but I'm pretty sure the Miss Victoria inheriting the plantation was an oddity. If I recall my history lessons, property, especially on this scale, was always left to the nearest male relative. The thinking being that a woman wouldn't be able to handle the responsibility. So, my dearest one who can handle any and all responsibilities, why did Victoria get all the goods?"

Wiggling a bit, Mae smiled. "Only you could find a mystery within a mystery. Is that relevant? Do you think her father killed her boyfriend so he wouldn't get his farmer hands on Harris's land?

Dash put the book down and wrapped both arms around his wife.

"Right now, I'm going to think of other things," he said as he kissed her.

CHAPTER SEVEN

After attending Mass the next morning and breaking their fast with the sisters, Mae, Billy, and Dash, son again perched on his shoulders, decided to stroll the grounds in the bright sunlight. They were to meet Miri Pat in an hour in her office to complete their plotting.

The graveyard didn't look very menacing now. T.J. got down so he could explore the tombstones and examine the ground for footprints. They continued their walkabout heading down the road behind the church and the motherhouse.

"What's here that I'm missing?" asked Mae. "I mean what is someone after if someone is after something? This is a beautiful place, but really. Buried treasure, buried bodies. I mean we've just come from the graveyard and there aren't any disturbed graves."

Dash stopped and swept his arm across the vista. "Land, Maevis, land. Most wars are fought over it. This is prime real estate. Tear down the buildings and there is plenty of room for high-end homes. Don't tear them down and convert the buildings into condos, more retirement space. Unless I'm mistaken, some of that has already taken place when the old dorm rooms were converted to apartments. Remember the aging of America."

Billy interjected, "Remember the Maine. Those baby boomers have to go someplace. This could be a paradise for them."

"What about the sisters who live here now?" Mae asked, frowning.

"There's not that many and they won't last long. Sad reality," Billy said.

"On that dismal note, let's head back to the guest house and sit for a minute before we have to put on those good old thinking caps our teachers told us we had."

"Lead on, Doctor Summers. Lead on." Billy pointed toward the house.

The adults sat in the living room feet stretched out, consuming warm beverages. Dash read aloud from the pamphlet so all would know the history of Marianwood, the proper name for the motherhouse and grounds.

T.J. went to the bedroom to fetch his backpack full of art supplies so he could entertain himself while the tall folks gabbed.

Suddenly he stormed into the room, a look of alarm on his face. "Daddy, we have an emergency!" His bottom lip quivered as he started to tear up. "Petey Rabbit is gone. The goblin took him or maybe it was the ghost. I just know she did. Why didn't you stop her?"

"Petey is missing from where? And take a deep breath, son. I told you there are no ghosts and no goblins. Even if there were, they don't take stuffed rabbits. I'm no Ned Parker, but I do know that."

"Mommy and I made the bed this morning and I tucked him into the covers while we went to church. I told him I'd get him, and he could come with me now." Tears ran down his face.

Mae jumped up. "That's what we did. Okay, no tears. He's here somewhere. We'll find him. Let's go upstairs." The adults followed and began looking high and low for the stuffed rabbit. The backpack was dumped out on to the table and searched. The once neat bedroom torn apart. Uncle Billy's room was next. No rabbit.

The search moved downstairs. In the kitchen Mae looked through her medical bag while Billy pulled his briefcase apart. Dash went through his duffel bag of tools and sundry stuff. Billy got on his knees and peered under the table. When he stood up, he placed a small silver cylinder on the table.

"Is this what I think it is?" he asked Dash.

Dash picked the device up and studied it. "I do believe you are correct, cousin." He set it in the center of the table. Motioning for the others to be quiet, he said very distinctly into the eavesdropping device.

"Okay, listen up. You can mess with me, my wife, my cousin, and Sister Miri Pat but you do not mess with my son. I'm giving you one hour to return the stuffed rabbit. Now pay attention. The sound you are about to hear is my weapon being locked and loaded." He pulled the pistol from his belt, cocked it. A very definite unmistakable sound. "Hear that. One hour and then your ass is mine. You want it in a sling or a body bag?"

He put his finger over his mouth again and then motioned for the crew to gather their things, put on their coats, and move outside.

T.J. looked at his father. "You gonna shoot them for taking Petey?"

Dash's last words as they exited the guest house were "Damn right, son."

Outside they walked toward the prayer grotto opposite the guest house.

"The place is bugged, right?" asked Billy. "Think the rest of the motherhouse is as well?

"Makes sense. Miri's room and office for sure. They knew she called for reinforcements and heard T.J. introduce her to his best friend Petey last night. This is a probably just a warning to back off."

Mae tugged at his arm. "You can mess with my wife?

Was that necessary? And isn't the gun a bit of overkill?"

"Calm down, Maevis. I do have a plan." He pulled out his phone. "Grady, old chap, how's the best security man in these United States doing?" He laughed. "Yes, of course I want something, only advice for now. Listen up." Not only did Grady, Dash's former right-hand man in the Army, listen, but Mae, T.J., and Billy as well. "Guest house where we're staying is bugged. Need to find the nearest place to buy de-bugging equipment on a Sunday in Louisville." Dash explained finding the bug and the missing stuffed rabbit. A goodly minute passed when he nodded. "That's wonderful but by the time you ship it to me....Oh." He glanced at his watch. "He'll be here by five at the latest. You are the best. Tell him to go into Bardstown and text me. I'll meet him there and we can discuss how to handle this."

He handed the phone to T.J. "G-man wants a word with his little man."

T.J. took the phone and listened. He softly said, "Thank you, G-man. I love you." Handing the phone back to his dad, he told his mom, "G-man is going help us find Petey Rabbit. Said he'd come down to bust those bad men if he has to. Isn't he great, Mom?"

Dash looked at Billy and rolled his eyes.

Billy smiled. "Hey, this is just like the Magnificent Seven."

Dash turned to him. "Since there are only three of us, how do you figure that?

"Don't you see? First, there's us three, then you called in Irma and Ilene, now we're up to five and this guy Grady is sending makes six. Miri Pat makes seven and if we count the little guy, we're seven and a half." He began humming the movie theme.

Holding up his hands, Dash started to walk away. "Not even going to talk about that. I'm thinking we're more like the Apple Dumpling Gang. Come along, Mr. Briefcase. It's time to meet your sister, the one who asked us here so she can't be part of the seven. Did you ever really pay attention to that movie?"

Mae grimaced. "Looks like someone needs more food. Definitely sensing a refueling moment. Let's hope the kitchen is still open. Hell, I'll even cook you something."

Billy laughed. "Whose side are you on, Mae? Trying to poison him, are you?" He stopped in his tracks. "Let's order in pizza and some beers. What do you think, Dash?"

Dash shivered. "Left, right, left, right."

It was Mae's turn to laugh. She said to Billy, "You can take the man out of the Army, but you can't take the Army out of the man."

T.J. just shook his head at the mutterings of the grown-ups, but he did start with his left foot as he ran after his dad.

CHAPTER EIGHT

Dash pulled Billy aside as they entered the building. "Mae, you take T.J., and we'll meet you in a few minutes. In here, cousin." They stepped into an office off the corridor. He closed the door behind him.

"All right, William, what the hell is going on here? You're on the board of directors and Miri's brother so I assume you know something you don't want to share. Care to enlighten me?"

"I hate to disappoint you but, at this moment, you know as much as I do which is everything Miri told us. I'm with you on the eavesdropping devices, but not sure why someone needs to know what she's doing. And also not sure about the voices or who might be moving her things and Petey Rabbit around."

Dash studied Billy and decided he wasn't holding back. "Are you privy to whatever plans Miri might have to save them from financial ruin? As I said to Mae, this land must be worth a good penny or two. And, this really hurts to say, I think some, possibly all of this, is an inside job."

"Let me get this straight. You think one or more of the sisters are out to get my sister?" Billy asked. "Nah, you're barking up the wrong tree. These women aren't the devious type."

"Never met a woman who didn't have a bit of deviousness in her, religious or not. You're just blinded because of Miri Pat – the essence of goodness. Trust me, I've been involved with a few more women than you. Well, actually that number would only have to be two to be ahead of you in that department."

"Can I help it if I'm a one-woman guy? A guy who stayed home rather than gallivanting around the globe whether under the auspices of Uncle Sam or on his own dime—well, more like nickel." Billy pushed past his cousin. "Speculation, dear colonel, will get us nowhere. Let's meet my sister and get down to work."

They texted Sister Miriam Patrice to meet in the dining hall. When she arrived, she asked, "I thought we were going to meet in my office. What's going on?"

"Sit down, my sister dear, and let me tell you a tale." Billy laid out the latest plan.

She sat back in her chair. "Oh dear, someone called Jumbo Washington is coming down to help. Will he have a gun? Is Irma bringing her gun? We're not that far from Fort Knox. Should I just call over there and ask for some artillery?"

She reached over to T.J. "I'm sorry about Petey, little guy. Don't worry, we'll find him."

Standing, she said, "Let me run to my office and get the rest of the stuff you asked for. Be right back. I take it we're going to work in here."

"Any food around, so I can feed the starving beast known as my husband?" Mae yelled after her.

"Going to order pizza, sis. What kind of topping do you want?" Billy called out. Miri answered that the luncheon being prepared was so much better than pizza, so hold off.

Mae reached into her voluminous purse and pulled out peanut butter crackers, handing them to Dash and her son. Billy waved her off.

Dash and T.J. carried drinks over to the table. "Coffee

for Uncle Billy and Mae. Milk for T.J. and me."

Billy, still fussing about pizza, decided it would be for dinner that evening. "Think twenty will be enough? Figure the good sisters could use a treat."

"Not to mention a boost in their blood pressure and cholesterol. The only one in the room pizza won't hurt is Thomas, at least not right now." Mae shook her head.

They looked up to see Miri Pat practically running into the room. She waved Petey Rabbit. "Look who was sitting on my desk. All he needed was a card saying, 'Message Received.'"

T.J. jumped up to grab the rabbit and hug it. He then hugged Sister, thanking her for saving his Petey. Turning to his father, he said, "Look, Daddy, Sister Miri Pat saved Petey. Isn't she wonderful?"

Dash sighed, once again getting no credit for his part in saving the world or even just saving Petey Rabbit. Instead, he nodded in agreement. "She is that, son, wonderful with a capital W."

"Put Petey in your backpack and don't let him out of your sight. Wonder who's next on the 'mess with' list. Whatever happened to my quiet weekend getaway?" Mae moaned.

After working on their individual projects for as long as they could, they headed upstairs to the offices for more records. Dash and Billy did a quick search for bugging devices. Not finding any didn't mean some weren't there, so a warning to watch what was spoken aloud was issued.

Dash settled at the long table situated in the meeting room between Sister Miriam Patrice's office and that of her assistant, Sister Annalise. His first priority was to review the work charts of the full-time staff and those day-laborers brought in as needed. He wanted an idea of how many outsiders would be on the grounds at any time, specifically the names and duties of those working yesterday. Who had access to the guest house?

Billy listed all the latest improvements to the site and then compared the various jobs with the list of workers. With no known motive, it was a long shot that one of the casual laborers was doing the pranks as Dash decided to label them. Since it was his sister who was the main object of these jokes, Billy was leaving no stone unturned.

Sister Annalise came into the office, surprised to see the guests hard at work shuffling papers. Maevis greeted her and waved her over to her portion of the table.

"Sister, I understand that you work closely with the retirement home. Could I bother you to help me cross-reference the residents' names with the visitors' logs for both the home and motherhouse?"

"Yes, my uncle lives over at the home, so I'm over there just about every day either visiting him or checking to see all is well with everyone. They are part of our community, if you will." She peered over Mae's shoulder. "What are you looking for? Is there a problem that I should know about?" She looked toward Miriam Patrice's office.

Mae wasn't sure how to answer. The one topic no one had touched upon was who should know what. Was Annalise a trusted ally, one who wouldn't judge Miri Pat harshly for hearing voices?

Fortunately, she was saved when T.J. tugged at his mother's sleeve. "Mommy, I have to pee. Do you know where the bathroom is?"

Maevis looked at Annalise. "Which direction? I'm assuming there is a public restroom on this floor."

"Assumption correct." She walked to the door and pointed down the hall. "There's one in the hallway beyond the drawing room. You can either go down this hall and take a left or cut through the drawing room, head toward the right and you'll see a passage to the hall and restroom. Do you want me to show you the way?"

Taking T.J.'s hand, Maevis shook her head. "No, not

that far. If I get lost, we'll be back."

They waved at Dash, but he didn't see. Head down, he concentrated on the sheets in front of him.

Yesterday when they had a quick tour of the ground floor, it had been almost dark, and they could barely make out the furnishings. In the bright sun, the drawing room stunned Maevis. Tall, mullioned windows with large floral print curtains that matched the fabric on the love seats scattered throughout the room. Each end of the room had a massive piece of furniture: ornately carved buffets. Tall vases filled with elaborate floral arrangements graced each end of the pieces with the center displaying porcelain figurines. The hardwood floor had several matching rugs spaced to create little sitting areas. The overall effect was right out of *Architectural Digest*. Maevis stopped to read the various plaques explaining the history of the pieces and the date of donation by families of the sisters or others thankful for the prayers of the congregation.

Dancing from one foot to the other, T.J. tugged at his mom. "Remember I have to pee."

The restroom was indeed off the hall at the far end of the drawing room. Fitting in with the old milieu, the stalls were wooden. Again, the room was a step back in time, old fashioned but pristine.

T.J. took care of his business, and his mother helped him wash his hands.

"Wait here," she said.

T.J. stepped into the hall and immediately walked over to the stained glass insert in the door at the end of the hall. Flowers and books grew in a garden. A tree in the background had books for leaves.

He opened the door. Enchanting. The room, bathed in sunshine, had a rainbow of colors streaming through stained-glass windows. He walked slowly to the first window where a young girl sat reading, a black puppy by her side. "It's just like me and Pansy Pup," T.J. said as he ran his fingers over the bottom of the insert.

He scanned the room and saw two sisters sitting at the far end doing what the room intended. Suddenly he remembered his mother. He was supposed to be outside the restroom, and she would be upset to find him gone.

CHAPTER NINE

When Mae exited the stall, she didn't see T.J., but figured he was outside in the hall. Stepping around the side of the stalls to reach the sink at the far end, Maevis washed her hands. Head down, she felt a presence behind her and thought it was her son. Instead, as she glanced up, she briefly saw a gorilla standing behind her. Before she could scream, a large hand covered her mouth and a pillowcase was lowered over her head. A strong arm clasped her to a very solid body.

"Don't scream. I won't hurt you," a muffled voice said. The gorilla then picked her up and carried her out of the restroom. He unceremoniously dropped Mae on the floor behind a door in the drawing room. Banging her head as she went down, she lay stunned, unable to move.

T.J. opened the restroom door and looked inside for his mother. After searching everywhere, he decided she wasn't there. He ran through the drawing room looking this way and that.

"Daddy, Daddy, we have a catastrophe! Mommy's gone!" he shouted at his father.

Dash turned, taking off his glasses and pushing the papers to the side. "Say again."

"Mommy's gone. Really gone. The ghost got Mommy this time." He threw his arms into the air to indicate vanished.

Dash stood. "What? Gone from where?" He barely finished the question when a blood-curdling scream startled everyone except for the inhabitants of the graveyard.

He sprinted to the drawing room where he heard shouting and thrashing coming from behind a door. Billy followed with Sister Annalise. T.J. grabbed Sister Miriam Patrice's hand as they raced toward the sound.

"Stop struggling, Maevis. It's me," he said as he pulled his wife to her feet.

"Get this thing off me," she shouted at him.

"Again, stand still." He pulled out a knife from his utility belt and sliced through the cord, lifting the pillowcase.

Being free of the bag did nothing to calm his wife. She started to pound on his chest. "Say it again. 'Mess with my wife,' why don't you?" She stepped back and held out her hand. "Give me your gun. Now."

The audience of the older sisters and their Sunday visitors who had gathered stood in stunned silence.

"Doctor Summers, get a grip. No way are you touching my weapon. Take a deep breath and tell me what happened. You can do that, can't you?"

She cast him a look that would curdle milk, stop a clock and any number of other things.

"I don't want to shoot you, just the gorilla who did this to me."

"Gorilla?"

"Yes, the man had a gorilla mask on."

Billy looked at T.J. "Did you see a gorilla?"

"No sir. Nothing. Just no mommy."

Dash turned to the audience. "Ladies, we're looking for a gorilla mask. A little help here. Keep your eyes open; search every trash can. If you see it, don't move it. Call Miri Pat, excuse me, Sister Miriam Patrice."

Seeing the looks on their faces, he continued, "Oh, you're in no danger. Some prankster has it in for me and my family." He smiled his sincerest. He led his wife to a loveseat and forced her to sit. Billy pulled up a chair to sit opposite them while T.J. and Miriam Patrice hovered nearby.

Billy started. "Maevis, sweetheart, can you tell us calmly what happened.?"

She took a deep breath. "You wouldn't be calm if someone put a bag over your head. I thought he was going to kill me. He said he wasn't going to hurt me, but he did anyway. I mean by dropping me. I hit my head." To confirm this, she reached up and rubbed her head.

Dash asked calmly, "Mae, can you describe your attacker?"

"What about 'gorilla' don't you understand? Don't push, because I'm very close to losing my temper."

"Really. I hadn't noticed. Now, Maevis, how tall? My height?"

"No, just a few inches taller than me or so it seemed with the mask on."

Dash pulled her up, spun her around and wrapped his arms around her. "Close your eyes. Describe his body type. Skinny, fat?"

"Solid, I'm thinking you'd say, kinda fullback. Arms thicker than yours. Steel-like. Smelled of moldy cigarettes." She turned to face him. "What does it matter?" She collapsed onto the loveseat.

Dash changed the subject as he leaned over to examine her scalp. "No blood, no broken skin." He turned her face so he could study her eyes. "Don't think you have a concussion, but we might go to the ER and have you checked out."

Mae swatted at his hand. "I'm the doctor here, and I'll determine if I need to go see another one." She narrowed her eyes to glare at her husband. "One more time, Colonel, mess with whom?"

Looking over at his cousin, the intrepid lawyer, Dash asked, "You still have those divorce papers? Thinking we might need them now." Turning to his wife, he scoffed, "Give over, Maevis. So some guy in a gorilla mask scared you. You're fine now, aren't you, Doctor Summers? Stop whining. We have work to do, sweetheart. Are you up for it or do you want to go back to the guest house and have a lie down?"

"By myself, alone, after I was attacked? What do you think?" She pulled herself up off the settee, straightening her clothes. "Damned if some gorilla, literal or figurative, is going to get the best of Maevis Summers." She reached for T.J.'s hand. "Let's go. We're going on a gorilla hunt." And she marched off singing a variation of "Going on a lion hunt."

Eyes wide open, T.J. looked back at his father, pleading for help. He held on for dear life as his mother dragged him away.

Billy started laughing and shook his head. "Your finesse with women, especially that woman, amazes me. No mollycoddling for you. If you are ever found dead in your bed, the cops won't have to look very far. One of these days, my dear cousin."

Sister Miriam Patrice sat down next to Dash. She took his hand. "Brings back a lot of memories of when you three were little kids. You know what strings to pull with each other. A little sympathy for these non-combat veterans would help here, Dashiell, if I may add my two cents."

Dash growled. "Memories are false, old lady." He shook his head. "This is just a little wake-up call. She's the one who insisted we come since, after all, 'it's Miri Pat'. Here we are, and now she needs to stand up and be counted."

Dash rose to his feet. "That being said, I better find them before she accidentally pulls T.J.'s arm off. You saw the bad husband; now I'll be the good husband and give her a shoulder to cry on."

CHAPTER TEN

The Reading Room was where he found them. He looked at the beautiful stained glass insert in the door, just the thing to entice a child to wander in. He opened the door slowly so he wouldn't disturb any of the good sisters who just might be doing what the plaque on the door said.

Mae and T.J. sat at a table close to the door. While Mae sat with her head in her hands, T.J. stared at the stained-glass windows. The only other occupants were two sisters at the other end of the room reading quietly, oblivious to the commotion of a few minutes ago.

Dash sat down next to Mae and put his arm around her. "Hate me?" he whispered.

"No, more like disappointed in myself. Panicking like I did. Whatever happened to all that self-defense training you gave me over the years? He shouldn't have been able to get the pillowcase over my head so easily."

Shrugging, Dash said, "Don't worry about it. The element of surprise is a mighty leveler in a fight. You sure you're okay?"

She nodded, and then turned to face her husband. "Just what do you think is going on? Are the sisters in real trouble or is this just some mad prankster upset that we showed up?"

Dash shrugged. "Don't know the answer to that. Billy and I agree that what was going on with Miri Pat is an inside job." He held his hand up. "Meaning staff, not the other sisters. Your being accosted by a man changes things. Escalation."

Both of the sisters at the other end of the room turned to look at the family.

Turning to them, Dash said, "Apologies, Sisters. We're leaving now, so quiet will resume. Come on, T.J. Let's go to the dining hall and see if there is any available ice cream. I know it's not the usual snack time, but I think we could use to re-fuel a bit."

T.J. spoke up. "Daddy, isn't this the mostest beautiful room in the world? All these pretty windows."

Dash looked at the stained-glass windows, sun streaming through. "Yes, son, yes, it is the mostest beautiful room in the world."

They stopped by Miri Pat's office to invite the rest of the team to follow. Billy was the only one interested in a snack. Since the dining hall was open all day, any sister desiring a quick sweet snack would not be disappointed. And the ice cream machine was self-serve, so that's what they did.

T.J. acted as a waiter and relayed their requests to Dash, who operated the machine. Once everyone was licking their cones, T.J. said, "Daddy, I've been thinking about this. When I left the bathroom, I didn't see anyone in the hall, or I wouldn't have left Mommy alone. And I didn't hear anyone on the stairs right outside the room with the beautiful windows. So where do you think this gorilla man was hiding? He should have had on a ghost mask to make it really scary. Right, Mommy?"

Mae crunched on the cone, having eaten all the ice cream. "Honestly, Thomas, the gorilla mask was scary enough. Just so sudden. Wonder if he was in the bathroom waiting for someone to come in? I mean, if he was watching us, he had to figure we'd be needing a bathroom break at some time, especially if he counted the number of cups of tea I drank. He wasn't after Dash or Billy since they would be more trouble than me. No, fairly certain he was after me. Remember the sequence: my wife, my cousin, even me."

Billy stuffed his cone in his mouth and mumbled something which could have been "you're not just a pretty hat rack."

Dash reached over to Mae. "How bad is your headache? And don't say you don't have one. Remember me? The king of concussions."

She got up and began wiping the drips and drabs off T.J.'s mouth and chin. "I'll take an aspirin. If that doesn't do the trick, I'll find a quiet corner. Not going to the guesthouse alone just in case I'm wrong about Billy being next."

"Mae, you got it wrong. I said they could mess with me, my wife, my cousin, and even Miri Pat. No, they're not going in any order except vulnerability." Dash licked his lips and began to clean the crumbs from the table.

Billy made himself another cone. "If that were the case, I'm next. These guys, if they are guys and not gals, aren't stupid. Would you mess with the man carrying the loaded gun? No, I suspect they will jump me next and beat me soundly with my briefcase."

T.J. said, "Oh, no, Uncle Billy. I'll stick with you and bust 'em if they try to hurt you."

"My little hero," Billy said as he devoured the second cone. He started for a third when Dash grabbed him.

"Leave some for the sisters, you ninny."

"Fear makes me hungry," Billy said.

Dash pulled at his cousin. "No, it makes you stupid." He clapped his hands. "Everyone back to work. It will be lunchtime soon and it would be nice if we actually had a fact or two relevant to the case by then."

"If only we knew what was relevant..." Mae muttered.

CHAPTER ELEVEN

The noon bell tolled just as Mae was about to put her head down in defeat. Damn him. Dash was correct in that she needed to be examined. Even a mild concussion should be properly handled.

As they filed out of the office, Dash put his arm around her. "Looking a bit pale there, Wonder Woman. After lunch how about we ask Sister Miri Pat if you can use her bedroom to rest for a bit. What do you think of that?"

Hearing this, Sister caught up with the couple. "I'd be happy to lend you my room. It's a single bed, so if the little one wants to crash with you it might be crowded but you are welcome."

They waited until the rest of the sisters had filed through the dining line. When it was their turn, they filled their trays. Sunday lunch was roast beef, mashed potatoes, broccoli or beans with a gelatin or a green salad. A vegetable casserole was available for those who preferred a vegetarian diet.

Miriam Patrice looked at the men's plates. "There is plenty, so don't be shy. The cook would be pleased to see you chowing down. She works very hard to make tasty dishes, but I fear most of us are not a worthy audience."

Dash, Mae, T.J. and Miri Pat found a table and were about to pull up a chair for Billy when they saw him take a seat at the next table where Sister Annalise sat. She was one of the younger women, full of energy and ideas. Medium height and slim of build, she waved her hands around when she talked. The conversation lasted all through the meal.

"'Curiouser and curiouser,' as your brother likes to say. Wonder what the counselor is up to?" Dash whispered to Miri Pat.

Mae smiled. "If Billy ever stops eating, you can ask him."

When they all finally had their fill, Dash stopped his cousin while he was collecting plates to return them to the kitchen. "Are you making new friends? What were the two of you talking about? Thinking it seemed intense for a Sunday lunch. Or were you just practicing that renowned cross-examination skill of your?"

Billy winked. "A little bit of everything. When we met last year, she was very reserved, almost timid. So I prodded and probed. She's full of ideas, if only one asked her, which was my number one mission. Find out what's behind that quiet but very observant façade."

"You think she has anything to do with all this. Why? How?" Dash faced Billy. "Mae could have been seriously hurt, that's all I'm saying. Sisters might pull pranks, but this is going beyond a mere prank. And it had to be a man to, well, man-handle Maevis. She's no lightweight."

He watched and listened as his son spotted Sister Agnes Marie. The youngster waved at her and yelled, "Hey, Sister, you want to know something?"

The good sister put down her utensils. "Yes, young man, I do. What do you have to tell me?"

"We saw her. The ghost Victoria. Last night when we went for a walk. She was in the cemetery, and she waved at me. Daddy ran over to where he thought she was but," and here he threw his hands into the air, "Bam, she disappeared. What do you think of that?"

"Really? You saw her? You're not teasing an old woman, are you?"

T. J. shrugged. "No, Sister, my daddy wouldn't like

that. No, really, really, really. I saw her with my own two eyes." He pointed to them. "And I don't need glasses!"

Sister Agnes Marie smiled. "I need to talk to your daddy. You really saw Victoria. I'll need to record this sighting in my notebook. One day I'll publish it and you will get a copy. You'll be in it. Might need to get your photograph. What do you think of that, young man?"

T. J.'s eyes grew large. "Really? Wait 'til I tell the kids at school. Bet they're not in a book." He trotted off to tell his parents the news.

Mae mulled over Miri Pat's offer of a bed as she ate slowly. Dash still wanted her to go to the ER or an Urgent Care for another opinion, quoting 'Physician, heal thyself.' She reached across the table to take Miri Pat's hand. "You and Dash are right. I need to rest."

The women walked down the third-floor corridor where most of the sisters lived. The very elderly or infirm sisters lived in the new care area on the other side of the motherhouse. For them, a nurse was available within a moment's notice.

Miri Pat pulled out a single key and unlocked her door. "Locking the door is so unusual, but after my prayerbook was moved Friday, I decided it might be a small deterrent." She flung the door open and let Mae enter first.

Mae smiled at the very tidy room. She crossed to the bed and sat down. Kicking off her shoes, she said, "I can't thank you enough. Dash doesn't show it, but he is worried about me. We've come a long way together, and now we have the little one to think of. Cements everything. Lock me in if you want. I'll rest for about a half hour and then I should be good to go."

Miri Pat tossed Mae the key. "Lock yourself in. If, God forbid, there were an emergency and you couldn't get out, I'd never forgive myself. And we don't even want to think what Dash would do."

Miri Pat was halfway out the door when she turned. "If you hear voices, you'll understand what I've been experiencing. Though I'm not sure that phase of the whatever is going on hasn't been stepped up a notch."

As Dash and Billy were leaving the hall, an elderly sister, older than Agnes Marie, stopped them. She pulled on Dash's sleeve as he passed her table. "Are you the soldier?" she asked.

"Yes, S'ter," Dash answered reverting to his grade school days at St. Mary when saying the full title was more trouble than he wanted to take.

"Come closer. You're a big one for sure," she said, squinting up at him.

"I prefer tall to big," Dash said as he squatted down next to her.

"May I touch your face? I can only see objects very close to my face, but I can figure out how things look by feeling them. I'm Sister Bernadette, the oldest at ninety-seven, so everyone pampers me by acquiescing to my wishes."

Dash reached for her gnarled hand, guiding it to his face.

"My mother had a friend who was blind from birth. She always asked us kids if she could 'see' our faces by touching us. Never sure what she got from it, but who was I to ask or argue?" Dash said.

Sister Bernadette felt his beard. "Nicely trimmed. Neat. Military-like, I guess." She pulled his face closer to hers. "Ah, blue eyes. You've a good face. How's your head after the accident? I remember Miriam Patrice asking us to pray for your recovery."

Dash took her hand and placed on the right side of his head. "Can you feel the slight dent in my skull? Thanks to your prayers and the help of my family, I am able to function, almost up to par."

She released him but not before whispering. "I'd like to

talk to you alone. Soon. You're here to fix things, right?"

He responded quietly, "Yes, I hope I can. Anytime. Just send someone to fetch me."

Standing he bade her goodbye.

Out in the hall, he said to Billy, "Sharp old lady, and she knows something is wrong. Hopefully, she'll talk to me sooner rather than later. Back to the grindstone, old man."

CHAPTER TWELVE

Mae stretched out, covering her feet with the small quilt folded neatly at the foot of the bed. She thought about searching the room for listening devices, but her eyes closed before she could move. She definitely needed to head into town for a quick x-ray when she got up.

Muffled voices, but someone talking somewhere, interrupted her sleep. Without moving she concentrated on the sounds. She strained to understand the words when another sound caught her attention. She glanced at the doorknob. Someone was turning it ever so quietly. She grasped the key, stuffing it in her pocket. She stretched over to the desk and grabbed a marble bookend. Sliding out of the bed, she moved silently to stand behind the door. This time the element of surprise was going to be on her side.

Billy looked up from his notes to glance around the room. "Dash, where is T.J.?"

Dash studied the room. Petey Rabbit peeked out of the backpack which hung over a chair at the end of the table. Throwing down his pen, he asked loudly, "When did he leave? I'm going to kill that kid."

"No, you're not. I bet he went to the bathroom." Billy pushed his chair back and walked out of the room.

Overhearing this, Miri Pat walked to Dash's side. "You don't think he went looking for the gorilla man, do you?"

"No, more likely, he went in search of Mae. Wonder if he heard you tell me where your room is? Listen, would you look for him there? I'm going with the same statement from last night that I shouldn't be prowling around where you and the sisters sleep."

"Will do. I'll call you if I find him. What are you going to do?"

"If you're going up, I'm heading down. If he eats anymore ice cream, he will burst." He felt like he was going to swear so he clamped his mouth shut. After nodding at Miri Pat, he turned to Annalise and said, "Sister, you hold the fort here. If he returns, tell him to glue the seat of his pants to that chair and then call her." He pointed at Sister Miriam Patrice.

Billy ran into Dash as he headed down to the dining room. "No kid in the drawing room or bathroom or reading room. Where are you heading? Ice cream temptation, you think?"

"Hoping so. Miri Pat is heading up to her room, so we'll head down. If he's not at the ice cream machine, we'll explore the nether regions." He sighed. "Is parenthood always this hard, or is it just that I'm old?"

Billy laughed. "A bit of both, old man. Biggest problem is he takes after you — fearless Fosdick."

When T.J. wasn't devouring more ice cream, the men started to reconnoiter the lowest level. Exiting to the right, they walked down a hall which led them to the church. Convenient if it rains, no walking outside.

Slowly opening the door, Dash half-called, half-whispered his son's name, causing several sisters who were praying to turn around. He apologized and explained the reason for the disturbance. They responded saying no short person had been seen or heard by them.

As they left, Billy said, "I bet he's hiding in there somewhere, thinking this is all a game."

Frowning, Dash shook his head. They backtracked past the dining hall heading in the other direction. They passed the closed kitchen, locked tightly.

Billy pointed ahead and said, "If I remember the plans correctly, this passage leads to the retirement center. Again, a convenient way to get to the dining hall or church without encountering the weather. Actually, a clever idea for the older folks. Wonder if I should talk to Miri Pat about moving Mom here?"

"Bet your sister has already talked to her about that. This place isn't as warm as Florida, but she would be closer to all her brood. Surprised Owen and Tom didn't consider this place."

Billy snorted. "As if your father and uncle would leave Clover Pointe now that little Thomas is there. I've seen Owen look at his grandson. Your redeeming feature for sure. And I'll admit a soft spot for the little guy."

"The little lost guy."

They reached the connecting doors to the retirement center. Locked. Turning back, they decided to check out the laundry room. Unlocked—an anomaly. All was quiet since it was Sunday, but a line of rolling bins of laundry sat ready for Monday's shift. Dash pulled the clothes out of them to make sure T.J. hadn't climbed in.

They checked the door to the mechanical room which housed the boiler for heat and other machines that helped the household run smoothly. Again, locked.

At the closest stairway, they climbed to the main floor. Dash pulled out his phone to call Miri Pat. No answer. Nodding toward the staircase, he said, "We're going up. I don't care how many rules this breaks."

The men took the stairs several at a time. When they reached the second floor, they stopped long enough to call for T.J. No answer but they continued to call as they opened any closed doors, peering in hidey holes for a four-year-old. Nothing.

"Onwards and upwards," Billy announced as they ran up to the third floor. This time they called out for Miri Pat.

She stuck her head out of her room. "Over here."

The men jogged down to her. "Anything? Please say yes," Dash said.

"Unfortunately no, on all fronts. No T.J. and no Mae. All that's left are her shoes." Miri Pat held these up before tucking them into her large pockets. "I've tried her phone and no answer."

Dash said, "Hates to carry it but is very quick to hassle me if I don't have mine." He stepped back into the hall. "Here's the plan. Miri Pat, you head that way and check every room. Billy, take the corridor over there. I'll head down the hall in the opposite direction. Meet at the junction."

Billy interjected, "This reminds me of another movie: And Then There Were None."

Dash glared at him. "Move, William, before I 'none' you."

The search began. It wasn't long before they met at the crossroads of the hall.

"Miri Pat, what's down there, behind that door?"

"Not much, just a storage area. It seems like a million years ago when the community first began, the sisters often boarded girls, even as young as five or six." Sweeping her hand toward the rooms they had just investigated, she continued. "This was one big dorm filled with beds and small dressers. The rest of the girls' things, seasonal clothes, lockers, etc. were kept in wooden closets in that room."

When she stopped talking, they heard a muffled cry. Turning toward they door, they could hear the urgent, "Daddy, Daddy, is that you?"

Dash ran to the door, but it wouldn't open. "T.J. stand back I'm going to kick the door in."

Billy hurried forward, key in hand. "Hey, Rambo, try this. Remember the thousand and one keys. Well…"

The door opened and there stood T.J., hands on his hips and a frown on his face.

Dash bent down to hug his son. "If I hadn't been so

worried, I'd, I'd… well I don't know what I'd do. Why the devil did you wander off? How many times…"

T. J. held up his hand. "I did tell you, but you had your nose in your work, just like Mommy says you do."

"Did you whisper to me? Because I don't remember hearing you speak out loud."

Dash's stance mimicked that of his son, hands on hips, frown on face. He heard Miri Pat say to her brother, "Now that reminds me of him as a little boy. Always confrontational. Ready with an explanation." She received a withering glare from the subject of her comment.

Stamping his foot, T.J. folded his arms across his chest. "Daddy, I need to tell you something. It's very important."

"Well, go ahead."

"Well, did you know Mommy is missing again? I went looking for her and she's not up here. That's when I went into this room. And, Daddy, the door wasn't locked. And I found something very important." His attitude was, "So, there!"

Billy stepped forward. "I won't comment about the apple not falling far from the tree. T.J., my darling little unlost boy, would you just spit it out for your old uncle? Unless, of course, what you found was a body. In that case, you can whisper to your daddy."

T.J. dropped his head. "Silly Billy. No body. Come here."

The adults followed him as he walked down the main aisle, stopping to point at something on the floor.

Billy stepped back, accidentally landing on his sister's foot. She promptly pushed him into Dash, who turned to again glare at his cousin.

Dash walked forward following his son. On the floor was a lump, brown and hairy looking. He knelt down, taking out a pen he poked at it. "T.J., did you touch this?"

"No Daddy, you said not to touch but to tell you where it is. I was trying to find you, but the door wouldn't open."

Lifting the gorilla mask off the ground with the pen,

Dash showed it to Billy and Miri Pat. "We all thought he went downstairs when he went up." He turned to T.J. "Did you look around? Did you think the man could still be here?" His tone was even though he wanted to scream at the child about the dangers of wandering these halls alone.

"Why aren't you scared?" Billy asked T.J. "Normal kids would have fainted by now or at least run screaming for their daddy."

T.J. stared at Billy. "Uncle Billy, my mama was a soldier. My daddy was a soldier. I'm going to be a soldier. We don't have time to be scared. Mommy is missing again, right, Daddy?"

Dash ignored the question, concentrating on the matter at hand. He turned to Miri Pat.

"I don't suppose you have a large bag in those voluminous pockets. And we need to find Mae. Not happy with this at all. And we need to alert your crowd about possible danger in the building. I don't suppose you have a way to assemble the troops, do you? Maybe Annalise could run around and gather them."

"Would an overhead announcement work? We gave up the bugle years ago." She reached for Dash's arm and T.J.'s hand. "We'll use the drawing room since half the sisters probably went to their rooms and the other half are down in the hall." She shook her head. "Billy, you can take orders for the pizzas and sides after we scare the bejeepers out of everyone. Just what they'll need, spicy food. A bit of a carrot at the end of the crooked stick."

T.J. pointed down the hall. "Sister, we can't go down those steps. The ghost will push us. Maybe that's what happened to Mommy. Maybe the ghost got her, not the gorilla man."

"Nonsense to the ghost stuff. No more, you hear. Double-time my friends, I have a wife to find, again."

CHAPTER THIRTEEN

Sister Miriam Patrice made the overhead announcement, trying to sound as cheerful as she could when she requested everyone's presence in the drawing room, no exceptions, no tardiness. The sisters slowly made their way to the room, talking quietly and shooting glances at Dash and Billy, surely the cause of this disruption to their serene Sunday afternoon.

Dash stood at parade rest. He was about to start when, out of the corner of his eye, he saw movement. He turned to watch Mae slowly inch toward a chair at the far end of the room. She was a bit disheveled and limping. She flopped into the chair.

T.J. broke ranks and ran to her.

"Excuse me for a moment, sisters. Talk amongst yourselves. Smoke 'em if you've got 'em," Dash said as he walked away, followed by Miri Pat. Billy apologized to the group.

Climbing into his mother's lap, T.J. grabbed her face. "Mommy, am I glad to see you. Wait 'til you hear what I found."

Dash positioned himself in front of his wife. "Maevis."

"Dashiell."

Billy walked up behind his sister and whispered, "A few words says it all." Miri Pat laughed.

"Mommy, listen to me. I found the gorilla man's mask,

but I couldn't find you. Daddy finally found me, but we still couldn't find you. Where were you?" The youngster, hands on hips, demanded an answer.

"Yes, Mae, please tell us where you were since you didn't stay in Miri Pat's bedroom," Dash said, mimicking his son's stance.

Mae glowered at her husband. "Why don't you start with 'finally found'? My understanding would be that he too was lost." She sighed. "Dash, we have but one child, not six or seven wherein you might think one or two were expendable. One child." She held up one finger, which Dash kissed.

"Ah, Mae, you know I'd go looking for any number of our lost children. Let me correct that, unless it was the little girl with the red curls, the one with the big mouth, always telling me what to do or not do. That kid's on her own." He smiled prettily. "Maevis darling, what the hell happened to you?"

"Pretty dangerous words to the woman with curly red hair, the one holding the marble bookend," Billy piped up.

Dash held up his hand to indicate quiet. "Again, my dearest heart, what happened and then we'll discuss T.J. and his wandering ways."

Wearily, Mae leaned back in the soft chair, sinking deep into the soft cushions. "I fell asleep as expected but was awakened by voices, muffled to be sure but voices, nonetheless. These must be the ones you heard, Miri Pat. Just as I was about to search for the source, I noticed the doorknob turning. Grabbing the bookend, I moved next to the door. This time I was going to have the element of surprise. But the door never opened. I listened carefully until I was pretty sure I could hear footsteps walking away from the room."

"That was probably T.J. looking for you, don't you think, Dash?" Billy asked.

Mae turned to T.J. "Why didn't you call out my name?"

Dash said sarcastically, "He probably did, but in a whisper like when he told me he was going to search for you.

Hard to know what he's saying when he does that."

Shaking her head, Mae continued, "Anyway, after a bit, I unlocked the door and decided to return to the office where I was sure all of you would be hard at work. I started down that dangerous staircase at the end of the hall. Yes, Thomas, the one with the ghost who pushes people. Well, no one has to push you if you have socks on which slip and down the stairs you go. Bumpety, bump."

"Ah, my graceful Gertie." Dash smiled at his wife.

"Again, Dash, she's still holding the bookend," Billy reminded his cousin.

"No broken bones. Didn't hit my head again. Black and blue all over; that's my doctor's opinion. I sat there contemplating my sins, for this trip must be punishment for something, when I heard the announcement. I dragged myself slowly here and now I'm going to take another nap, right here, right now." She gestured with her hand that they could all leave her in peace.

"T.J., you're in charge of your mother. Sit here; do not leave her or let her leave. And Mae, you're in charge of T.J. Do not leave him or let him leave. Got that."

Mother and son saluted as Miri Pat handed over Mae's shoes.

Dash, Billy, and Miri Pat returned to the assembly where Dash broke the news about an intruder in the building. He explained that no one, and he meant no one, was to leave the first floor unless it was to go to the dining area and then they were to travel in pairs. He was going to search the upper floors and would let them know when they might return to their rooms.

Turning to Miri Pat and Annalise, he asked, "I don't suppose you have a bunch of whistles you could pass out. Something to alert us of possible trouble."

The response was negative until one of the sisters raised her hand. "Miriam, I remember we bought a bunch of whistles and noisemakers for the summer fete last year. I bet some are still here. Shall I fetch them?" She waited for instructions.

"Wonderful, Sister. Annalise will go with you. Everyone please stay here until we find these whistles or noisemakers. Once Billy and I have cleared the rooms, you can move about. Again, I ask you to travel in pairs and lock your doors tonight. I assume you all have keys. Use them. Dismissed as soon as you have the whistles."

The group stood and saluted, half of them giggling.

Miri Pat faced Dash. "This is the most excitement they've had in years. How are the two of you going to search every place and be certain the culprit hasn't backtracked, or whatever one would do to stay hidden?"

Dash shrugged, "We'll solve that as we go."

Billy held his hand up and signaled for quiet among the sisters. "Don't forget I'm ordering pizza for everyone tonight. Think what toppings you want and salad, bread sticks, whatever you fancy." He pointed to Sister Agnes Marie. "Sister, would you please see what everyone wants? I'll get back to you shortly."

"Did I hear pizza?" Irma Tydie said as she and her sister stood at room's edge.

The assembly turned to look at the new visitors. Twins with a capital T, they wore matching pant suits, and their matching haircuts were achieved with a bowl over their heads.

Glancing to heaven, Dash said, "Thank God. Speak of reinforcements and they appear." He ran over to them lifting the diminutive women up to give a big hug.

Stepping out from around the corner, Marie Hammond, Dash's sister-in-law and often his nemesis, asked, "How about a hug for me?"

Wiping the shock off his face, Dash obliged. "This is a surprise." He looked behind her. "Don't suppose you conned your husband into coming? Could use another man or two."

Waving her hand dismissively, she said, "Sam's too

busy doing whatever it is he does to make the trip. I figured I should come along so Mae and Thomas don't have to drive back all by themselves. I know a toddler can be a distraction in the car."

Dash bent over to peck her cheek. "Ah, my very wise sister-in-law. Excellent." Billy and Miri Pat joined the group. "Marie, Irma, Ilene, you remember my cousin, Billy Mac. And this is his sister, Miriam Patrice. She is the high lama lama of the community right now. Miri Pat, you remember Marie, right?"

The first words out of Miri Pat's mouth were to Irma. "Did you bring a gun?"

Irma started laughing and then said to Dash. "Things going that well, are they?" Then back to Miri Pat, "No, didn't think I needed one."

"No, no, that's good. I've told Dash we don't allow guns on the grounds but he's insisting on carrying one." Motioning toward a sofa and chairs, she said, "Please let's find a seat so I can tell you myself what's going on and why we need reinforcements."

Dash pointed Marie in Mae's direction. "She could use a little attention."

"What did you do now?" Marie asked.

"Nothing, but that doesn't mean nothing happened to her. If she doesn't talk your ear off, T.J. will. Grain of salt, Marie, grain of salt."

Dash stood at the far end of the room. He watched as Billy compiled the pizza order and T.J. dragged his Auntie Re off to the dining room, certain she needed an ice cream cone after her long trip. The boy explained that he needed one after his adventure. Sister Miriam Patrice left with the Tydie twins for a tour of the building.

He sauntered over to the comfy chair where Mae sat smiling. He towered over his wife. Hands on his hips he said, "Well, my lady Mae, we are alone at last. Now, truth only, how are you feeling?"

"Slightly shaken, slightly stirred and definitely sore. I'm going to need some TLC, soldier boy." She sighed, patting the spot next to her on the over-sized chair. "Think you can sit here? A little cuddle would go a long way to healing my battered soul."

"Your wish is my command." He sat, putting his arm around her, saying, "Let's be sure we don't start anything that would embarrass either them or us. Take a deep breath. Again, should you visit the ER? Now that Marie is here, she can keep you company." He glanced at his watch. "Or we can go into town together. Grady's man should be arriving soon. Thoughts?"

She snuggled against him. "I'd love to oblige but no, don't want to answer questions about how I got these bruises and the bump on my noggin. That would remind me of the times I had to lie for that rat bastard of a husband. These bruises are too much like domestic violence. I've done an inventory while sitting here and my professional opinion is that nothing's broken, even sprained, just bruised. My head actually feels much better, thank you. No, I don't want to be sitting in some waiting room. I heard a rumor that pizza is on the menu tonight. Can't miss Billy being the lord of the manor passing out the pizza. Betcha he gets some beer as well."

Dash laughed. "I thought I'd pick up some when I go to meet Jumbo. Can't wait to see him. I never think of Grady as having a sense of humor when he needs to be professional, but I'm sure he's having a good laugh about all this. Bugging devices and holy women, ghosts and goblins."

Mae started to pull herself up, but Dash stopped her.

"Not so fast. What happened upstairs? In the room? In the corridor?" He tilted his head to study her. "Not buying all of what you said. Not that you lied, but a sin of omission is still a sin."

She wrinkled her nose at him. "Okay, but you won't be happy. I was asleep like I said when I heard voices. I sat up to see if that helped my hearing. It didn't. Then I saw the doorknob turning. He or she shook it, asking if I was in there. Me, not Miri Pat. Muffled voice, but not a child's. Not a peep from this girl. Finally, I heard footsteps going away from the door. Adult footsteps unless Thomas was tromping around."

"Your take?"

Mae shrugged. "The gorilla man coming back for more. Someone knew I was in that room. Thank goodness Miri Pat gave me the key and I used it. After the footsteps were beyond hearing, I peeked out. All was clear so I darted for the staircase, ghost or not. It was the closest escape, and I took it. Forgot my shoes. Tripped on a step and tumbled down. I don't want to go the hospital or an urgent care. Again, injuries, if I have any, will look like a domestic and I'm thinking we have enough on our hands without wasting time trying to dispute that."

He smiled. "Tonight, in bed, I'll share my twisted thoughts about all this as I give you a good rubdown to ease the pain." He pulled her up to give her a hug. He looked to see Billy approaching. "Maevis, let's get you downstairs to T.J. and Marie. I'll get the luggage out of the car and upstairs which is where I'm pretty sure Miri Pat will want our ladies."

CHAPTER FOURTEEN

As they carried the suitcases up the stairs, Dash looked at the keys Billy was jingling as he walked.

"Thought it might make sense to lock up as we cleared the rooms. Should we mark the doors, so we know where we've been?" Billy asked.

Dash said, "Excellent. We'll make a soldier out of you yet."

"Then let's do it."

An hour later the men had inspected the third floor, dropping off the luggage for Irma, Ilene, and Marie. They moved to the second floor which housed offices. Same routine: inspect the room and then lock it.

Just as they finished one side of the hall, Dash's phone pinged. Sister Bernadette desired his presence in the church. He hurried along and spotted her quickly. She sat in a corner near the front. He could tell by her posture that she was listening for him, so he called out to let her know he had arrived.

Dash entered her pew from the other side, so she didn't have to move. Sitting down, he leaned over to her and whispered, "You want to talk."

She grasped his hand. "Yes, yes, I do. I'm old and very blind but that doesn't mean I'm unaware of some strange things happening here. Not having much sight, I've developed the other senses a bit more. Please don't think this is the rambling of an old lady."

"No, of course not."

"When Miriam Patrice entered the community, I was in charge of the postulants and novices, so I've known her for over forty years. I've been her champion and pressed her to take the presidency even though she didn't want the job. Now I can sense something is wrong, but she won't confide in me."

Dash waited for more.

"Not only is something wrong with Miriam Patrice, but I confess to experiencing some odd things lately. Unexplained things. I fade into the background sitting here quietly. Unnoticed by most and I tell you someone has come into the church and done something that has caused a weird tapping noise to occur at odd times. Nothing consistent. And the smell of cigarettes. On someone's clothes, not that they are smoking in here."

"This last bit, the smell. When and where?"

"Different times and places. Many of us are very sensitive to the smell of tobacco, so anyone who works with us or around us or on our floor is told they cannot smoke or wear any clothing that smells of smoke, yet that is what I'm smelling. And not at times when the nurses or cleaning staff would normally be working."

"I assume that you haven't mentioned this to anyone. And why do you think something is wrong with Miri Pat?"

"Because I hold her hands when we talk and I sense a slight tremor, a tenseness. She's a grown woman, very competent so I'll not press her. What's going on, Colonel Hammond?"

He pulled in a deep breath. "Honestly, I'm not sure but something is. Have any of the other sisters experienced these odd happenings?"

"Several have mentioned hearing mumbling voices. Since many of us are wearing hearing aids, we assumed it had to do with that. At first, I thought the staff was messing about with something that triggered this. Others have complained about voices coming through their phones or computers. Ask Agnes Marie."

Dash squeezed her hand. "You don't know how helpful this is. Let me promise you that this will stop. Whatever mischief or malice is happening will end soon. You have the word of an officer and a gentleman." He stood to leave. "Rest easy, Sister, your burden is now my burden, and I will not fail you."

"Thank you, Colonel. If you need more, find me."

Dash exited the pew, genuflected toward the altar signing the cross as he rose. Always the altar boy.

Dash's phone pinged as he walked with Billy to the dining hall. Jumbo Washington arrived in town and wondered where they were to meet. That was a good question. He changed his mind about meeting in town and texted Jumbo to come out to the motherhouse but stop at the security hut. Dash would meet him there to explain the tasks ahead.

"Billy. I'm heading to the security hut to meet this Jumbo. You're in charge here. See what you can do to keep everyone together until the pizza arrives. Give me a head count when I get back. Think you can do this?"

Laughing, Billy said, "Just wait until you see what I have planned."

When they reached the dining hall, Dash retrieved Mae asking her if she wanted to come or stay for whatever floor show Billy had dreamed up.

Mae frowned and then twisted her mouth around before answering. "I want to meet Jumbo. Also think leaving this building will do my soul some good. Lead on, MacDuff."

They could hear Billy leading the sisters in song as they left the building. They strolled hand in hand toward the security hut speculating on what else Billy had up his sleeve. Laughing about the memories they shared of Billy's childhood productions to entertain the neighborhood.

"I never understood why he chose the law over the stage," Dash said.

"Money, silly. The law afforded him a very steady income from the moment he passed the bar. Have you ever observed him in court? An Oscar winning performance to be sure."

Dash unlocked the hut figuring it might not provide any warmth but would cut the breeze. Ten minutes later, a black Hummer pulled up, parked, and discharged the oddest couple ever. One man was the size of a giant, several inches taller than Dash and quite a few pounds heavier. The other man was only five-seven or five-eight at best but built like a fire plug. His muscles had muscles. Dressed all in black from military style boots to black hoodies, the men's attire shouted, "Don't mess with me!"

The shorter man stuck out his hand. "Colonel Hammond, I'm Jumbo Washington and this here is Tiny Muldoon. Reporting for duty, sir."

Dash waited in case they decided to salute. When they didn't, he put his hand out to shake Washington's and then Muldoon's.

"Gentlemen, a pleasure. This is my wife, Doctor Maevis Summers." He pointed to the hut. "Let's step into my office for a minute unless you think the Hummer has more room."

Tiny and Jumbo glanced at the hut and then each other. "The Hummer, sir." They returned to the vehicle and opened the doors.

Dash and Mae climbed into the back seat while the men resumed their seats up front. If nothing else, with the heater blasting, it was much warmer inside.

"Mr. Washington, or may I call you Jumbo?" Dash asked. "I'm sure Lennington told you why you're here. We need all the buildings swept for bugs and anything else that shouldn't be there. The sticking point is that this is the motherhouse for a community of sisters, most of whom are elderly. The head honcho, Sister Miriam Patrice, a cousin of mine, called us since she was hearing noises, voices and her belongings moved around. All this possibly in an effort to make her think she was, to put it in everyday parlance, losing it."

Tiny spoke up. "And you're sure she's not, losing it, that is. Any motive for these unusual circumstances?"

Mae held up her hand. "If I may interrupt, Mr. Muldoon, why are you called Tiny since you're obviously not? And you, Mr. Washington, Jumbo?"

"Pardon my wife, gentlemen, I can only assume that Grady gave you those nicknames. My wife isn't party to his peculiar sense of humor, and she often loses sight of the objective." He glanced at his wife whose facial expression dared him to continue. He didn't.

Tiny smiled a very broad smile. "The colonel there has it right. The major enjoys a topsy-turvy world. It would be too mundane for him to call me Jumbo and Jumbo to be called Tiny. Ma'am, if you like you can just call me Muldoon or Norman which is what my mom calls me."

"Norman it is." Mae said with a smile and then turned to Jumbo.

He shrugged. "The major isn't the only one with a sense of humor. I'm George Washington but prefer to be called Jumbo or Washington, ma'am, as there is nothing presidential about me."

"Jumbo it will be," Mae said.

"Well, now that we have all that sorted out, do you think we can return to the operation at hand? That being the de-bugging of all the buildings and a thorough search for the gorilla man." Dash glanced from man to man to gauge their reaction. "Let me explain about that." And he did so in great detail, starting with the disappearance of Petey Rabbit.

Norman turned to Mae. "Someone put a pillowcase over your head and dropped you on the floor. And stole a child's toy." He wiggled in his seat anxious to apprehend the miscreant. "Wait until I get my hands on him. He won't be messin' with no ladies or kids after that."

Jumbo put his hand out. "Slow down, Tiny. The colonel is in charge. Let's see what plans he has for us."

"I should have jumped in when we were reviewing names. Gentlemen, call me Dash, not colonel. Let's drive up to the guest house and you can begin by de-bugging it. Then we'll figure out who will sleep where, who takes first watch, and I'll have to do a perimeter check with both of you so you can see the scope of the operation."

Mae jumped in. "Have you gentlemen eaten recently?" She pointed out the window as the pizza delivery truck passed them. "I understand there is a rather large assortment of pizzas about to arrive." She turned to her husband. "How about we start at the dining hall and progress from there?"

CHAPTER FIFTEEN

The dining hall was buzzing. The sing-along had ended with a tap-dancing display by Billy and T.J. A number of sisters who had taken lessons years ago and remembered a step or two joined in. Everyone was smiling and laughing.

All that stopped the minute Dash, Mae and the black-attired men walked in. Silence was palpable.

Billy walked over to the quartet. "Well, you sure know how to kill a party." He held out his hand to Muldoon. "Welcome, Mr. Jumbo."

Muldoon said, "Sorry, but I'm Tiny. This here is Jumbo." And he pointed to his sidekick.

Billy's head swiveled back and forth between the new men. He finally sighed and flipped his hand. "Whatever!" He looked at Dash. "Are you all hungry? There's plenty of pizza and even a few beers. I set aside three Manly Meat pizzas for we manly men; thought there would be only three. Not sure if we have enough of those but plenty of regular pizzas."

"In a bit, William. First things first. He motioned for Jumbo and Tiny to follow him. Clapping his hands he said, "Sisters, these gentlemen are replacing the security staff until the Borland brothers can return. You won't even notice them as they search the buildings and roam the grounds. Still, if you ever feel in danger, blow those whistles or ring those noisemakers. Now please continue with your frivolity and enjoy the pizza."

Billy muttered, "Yeah, sure, they'll blend in, even

disappear, like the elephant in the room."

Dash shot Billy a look and then led the way to the table where Sister Miriam Patrice, Marie, T.J., and Sister Annalise were sitting. More one on one introductions.

Annalise volunteered to retrieve the Manly Meat pizzas from the kitchen while Billy set out plates and took orders for beer.

Dash waved him off. Rising, he said he was going to make himself a sandwich from the left-over roast beef. "You guys have at it with the pizza. When you're finished, we'll resume the mission." Saying he would join Mae at the other table, he left to wash up.

T.J. watched wide-eyed as the men made short work of the pizzas. Marie murmured something about hoping they didn't eat the table.

The men pushed back from the table and nodded at Dash. He beckoned them to join him. Miri Pat appeared. "Dash, where are these gentlemen going to sleep? And just what are they going to be doing?"

"Ma'am don't bother with anything. We're used to sleeping on the floor or ground. We've got our gear in the Hummer. You won't even know we're here if this is where we're supposed to be." He looked at Dash for an answer.

Dash jumped in. "I thought they could crash at the guest house. Not sure if you have a cot strong enough to hold them. We'll just throw some mattresses on the floor for them. Trust me, they are not used to being pampered."

After much to-and-froing, it was determined that Tiny and Jumbo would bunk in Sister Miriam Patrice's office. Mattresses from the upstairs storage area were retrieved, giving the men a chance to get a sense of the overall layout of the building. Tiny and Jumbo brought in their gear, dropping it on the floor. The Hummer parked for the night in front of the building for the time being.

"Now that we have the housing arrangements settled, gentlemen, time to go to work. Follow me over to the guest house and let's do some exterminating," Dash said as he pointed the way. "Miri Pat, tell Mae and Billy what we're up to, and we'll be back once we're done."

Dash stood back and watched as Jumbo and Tiny went inch by inch over the guest quarters. Since the building was small, the sweep for listening devices took under an hour. The experts found bugs, missed by Dash and Billy, in each of the bedrooms and the front sitting area.

"Now to the main building. If I'm correct, the office where you guys will be sleeping is also bugged. And you might ask Miri Pat if you can check her room. That's one of the places where she's heard voices. Figure there is some sort of transmitter there. Let me know when you want a tour of the grounds and the many doors that must be checked before this night is over."

Jumbo stepped up. "Sir, I think we should start outdoors and work our way in. Once we get warm, we're not going to want to go outside." Shivering, he added, "I brought my winter gear but, damn, it's worse than I thought."

As they toured the grounds, Dash's phone rang. It was Grady checking in.

"We're doing fine. The guest house has been de-bugged. Right now we're doing an outside tour, checking the doors, then we're moving inside to finish. Do you need to talk to them?" Dash asked.

He listened for a few minutes and rang off. "Bad news, guys. Grady turned meteorologist said there is the possibility of a nasty winter storm heading our way. Could shift and miss us, but then again maybe not. Let's head in and talk with Sister about what this could mean."

Sister Miriam Patrice met the men at the reception desk. "I didn't hear any 'it's eight o'clock and all is well.' Well, is it?"

Jumbo stepped forward. "Yes Ma'am, all is well. Now we'd like to see your room so you can retire without us interrupting you. Dash here says there might be a transmitter there causing you to hear voices and lose sleep. Can't have that, can we?"

"Fall in, men, and I'll lead the way. Dash, your crowd is waiting for you in the dining hall. I'm pretty sure T.J. is going to burst if he has one more cone. Mae is wilting fast so you need to get her back to the guest house and in bed, shouldn't be too hard since you've been doing that since you were teens."

Dash had the good grace to blush. He shook his head as he remembered all the kidding he has taken over the years about his relationship with Mae. From diapers and the playpen to marriage, divorce and re-marriage. Even now, after all the years and trauma, he couldn't help himself. He just loved to watch Mae move, talk and especially smile.

"Before we separate for the night, I had word a storm might be rolling in. How is your place fixed in case of an electrical outage? What's the backup?" he asked her.

"We'll be fine if I understand everything correctly. There are generators to handle the electric, if needed. Heat is on a boiler system and has never failed in the forty years I've been associated with this place. Hate to say it, but the guest house isn't as equipped. Would you want to stay here? I can get a room upstairs for Mae and T.J."

"Thanks for the offer, but we'll head to the guest house. Billy promised T.J. an evening of Disney movies and I need to make sure Mae gets some TLC. I'll call you if we run into some problem."

He saluted Miri Pat and headed to find his crowd as she called them. "Gentlemen, I will leave you in Miri Pat's hands. I'm just a phone call away. Keep the Hummer parked out front. Maybe it will be a deterrent from further high jinks."

Back in the guest house, the folks divested themselves of all the layers of clothes. Dash turned up the heat, trying to get some warmth into the old house.

"I'm going to take a long hot bath if anyone needs me. Implied message: don't need me," Mae announced. "Thomas, Daddy will get you ready for bed. Come here so I can give you your goodnight kiss. I'll see you in the morning." She bent down to kiss her son.

Dash kissed his wife. "Go, get upstairs, you look bushed. I'll lock up here and set things to right. T.J., head upstairs and get your jammies. We'll wash up in Uncle Billy's bathroom, okay with you, William?"

"No problem since the little guy is going to bunk with me. We just have to pick out the movies we want to watch. Want to join us, Daddy Dash?" Billy asked as T.J. jumped up and down, silently shaking his head no.

"I'd love to, but … Sure you want him in bed with you? He'll be a Mexican jumping bean after all the excitement of today." Dash asked.

"No problem. Had two jumping beans of my own a few years ago. Me and my buddy will be fine. I'll get him ready for bed. Are you going to do any patrolling tonight? Seems pretty cold. Who the hell would be out there if they didn't need to be? I can't believe whoever is doing this crap needs to do it right now," Billy watched his cousin mull this over.

Shaking his head, Dash answered, "Don't plan on going out unless summoned. Tiny is going to do rounds inside. I gave him the floor plans and marked the doors. If they're locked, he won't need to go outside." He started moving things around, setting the briefcase, the medical case, and his own bags on the floor. Glancing around, he said, "I'm bushed. Let's head up. And thanks, Billy, for taking the little guy. Mae and I could use a good night's sleep."

"Make sure that's what you do: sleep, I mean," Billy said with a wink as they climbed the stairs.

CHAPTER SIXTEEN

It was one a.m. when Dash made his way down to the first floor. The howling winds woke him. He needed to move around a bit, check things out. He stood looking out the front window when he heard someone coming down the stairs. Turning he saw Billy, shivering as he walked.

"Is the heat out? I'm freezing. Are you?" Billy asked.

"As far as I can tell, the heat's still on. Let me turn it up a bit. I'm afraid this is one drafty old house. Look out there. It's coming down like crazy. A regular blizzard. Really didn't expect this," Dash said. "You having trouble sleeping with the little one?"

"No, it's my stomach that's doing jumping jacks. Guess that pizza isn't setting too well with this aged body. Hate to say it, but that damned doctor wife of yours just might be right. How is she, by the way?"

"Sleeping like a baby. I slathered her with ointment. It's like sleeping with a tube of Ben-Gay. At least my sinuses are open. She took one of those pills that help you sleep if you are in pain." He stood at the window shivering himself. "I was going to send her and T.J. home today, but that's out." He pushed a curtain aside. "Listen, here that clink, clink. I think that's ice pellets hitting the window. Going to be a mess."

He motioned toward one of the chairs in the room. "Have a seat. How long do you think we'll need to be here? Not that I'm not loving every minute, but I do have responsibilities at home, as do you. No pending cases?"

"No trials for a few weeks. I've been making notes on those when I have a free minute. Not sure what Miri Pat thinks we're going to do. Find the gorilla man, I guess for one thing. Now that we know what's causing the voices and are pretty sure someone is moving her things around, I'm hoping she'll feel better," Billy said.

"And pray tell, why would she feel better knowing she's not crazy, but someone has her on their agenda? Why pick on her?"

Billy moaned, then shivered. "Wish we had a fireplace. Turn up the heat before I turn into an icicle." He stood up to hurry to the bathroom.

When he returned, he looked paler than before and was holding his stomach. "Damn, but this is inconvenient to say the least. What were you..." And he rushed away.

Dash frowned. Inconvenient for sure and definitely not good. He pulled up his duffel bag and rifled through it. Pulling out a small vial of pills, he set it on the table and poured a glass of water.

When Billy returned, Dash pointed to the pills. "Take one. Guaranteed by the U.S. Army to cure all ills. We carried these because what you have isn't just an inconvenience when you're living in the bush."

Billy followed instructions, groaning all the time. "Hey, could we table any further discussion until my gut stops gurgling. I think I'll head back to bed."

"Want me to get T.J.?"

"No, he's out cold, definitely exhausted. See you in the morning." With that, Billy climbed back up the stairs.

Dash tried to crawl into bed without waking Mae, but he was unsuccessful.

"Don't get in if your feet are cold. Not in the mood to warm you up," she said.

"You'll be fine; I've got socks on."

Mae started to laugh. "I bet you don't remember but

when we first started making love, oh so many years ago, you told me I couldn't get pregnant if you had your socks on. And I believed you."

Smiling in the dark, Dash said, "Well, I knew something was supposed to be covered. Just got the wrong body part. I'll keep my feet away from you, but get your butt over here so I can snuggle with you. It's like Doctor Zhivago's ice palace out there. We could be here until April!"

"Seriously, not that this isn't a beautiful place but…"

"My thoughts exactly. William owes us big time. Now to sleep, my beauty, so we can dig ourselves out of this mess in the morning."

"Daddy, Daddy. Wake up. Somehow, we got moved to the North Pole. Wake up." T.J. shook his father.

Dash pried his eyes open. "T.J., settle down. We're not at the North Pole, just looks like it." He squinted at his watch. Looks like it could be close to six. Happy morning.

Sitting up he pulled T.J. into bed with him. "Lord but you're cold. How long have you been up? Where's Billy?"

"I had to pee, so I got up and then looked out the window to see if Miss Victoria was walking around. But all that snow and wind. It's scary. Are we trapped inside?"

"You just snuggle with Mommy. Let me check this out."

Mae squealed when T.J. wrapped his cold hands around her. "What the…? Thomas, why are you so cold?"

Dash answered for his son. "That is what I'm going to find out. I know this is an old building, but it shouldn't be this cold."

CHAPTER SEVENTEEN

Annalise opened her door quietly. She looked up and down the hall to see if any of the other sisters were up. It was five-ish in the morning, not an unusual time for some sisters to rise. The howling winds and ice pellets hitting the windows kept them from getting a good night's rest. That was the case with Annalise.

Picking up her keys, she started down the hall to the spiral staircase. Normally she avoided it as potentially dangerous, a point proven when that visitor Mae fell down them yesterday. But today, time was of the essence and this staircase was closest to the door to the retirement home. And she needed to talk to her uncle in the worst way.

Annalise stepped out into a motherhouse wrapped in darkness with only the emergency lights to guide her. She knew the electricity was out, having heard the crack about two this morning. But she also heard the generators kick in, and they were purring along. That meant Miriam Patrice could be up and about as well as those two thugs assigned to guard the motherhouse.

Miriam Patrice could be a problem if she found Annalise up and about. Thinking her superior should be distracted by all that was going on, she wouldn't question Annalise's need to check on her uncle's welfare.

She reached the lowest level of the building. A long corridor connected the two buildings. A single door separated the two. Pulling out the key, she opened it and went on through to the elevator. Her uncle's room was on the top floor, and this would be the quickest way up. Not worried that anyone on this side of the building would question her presence she now picked up her stride.

All these rooms had once housed students who wanted a quality education without traveling to Lexington or Louisville. Once the college closed, the dorm rooms had been remodeled to make small apartments. On the first and second floor, two dorm rooms were transformed into suites that had one bedroom, a bath and a kitchenette opening into a small sitting room.

On the third floor, three or four dorm rooms made larger apartments, having two bedrooms in case guests came to visit. Annalise's uncle's room, 307, was one of the larger suites.

Annalise could see a light coming from under the door. She tapped lightly and then opened the door.

"Uncle Del, it's Annalise."

"I see. What are you doing up at this hour? Is there a problem? I saw the lights flicker, but nothing's gone down." Her uncle sat in his bed, comforters pulled up around his chin.

"Are you cold?" she asked.

"Not really. Just all that wind is making me think I'm cold. Must be freezing out there."

"That's why I've come." She nodded toward the spare room. "I don't suppose Tater is in there, is he? I haven't seen him since those guys arrived and I'm getting worried."

"Pull up a chair. To answer your question, I haven't seen Tater since the day before yesterday. I figured he was still hiding in the motherhouse. What's going on?"

Annalise started pacing rather than sitting. "Uncle Del, I don't know. Like you, I figured he found some hidey-hole and was there, but those guys that soldier brought in have, according to them, done a search top to bottom. Nothing found or so they told Hammond. I'm worried. Tater's not answering his phone."

Her uncle smoothed his covers. Patting the side of the bed, he again said, "Sit down, my child. It's likely that Tater went back to his place in town. When was the last time you saw him or talked to him?"

"I haven't talked to him since he pulled that gorilla stunt. He told me what he planned to do, scare the you-know-what out of the woman. He didn't intend to hurt her, but he dropped her and she banged her head hard. Now her husband is looking for revenge and I'm afraid when he does find Tater, he'll take his pound of flesh."

Del Boone, no relation to Daniel, shook his head. "Tater can hold his own, not against a gun but I've never seen a man beat him yet, except that damned chicken farmer. But sure that wasn't a fair fight. Next step, we need to get that gun from what's his name. Guys with guns don't know what to do without them."

Annalise stood up, shaking her head. "Don't think that applies to this guy, or to that giant he brought in. And how, in the good Lord's name, am I to take his gun away? He has it tucked away in his belt, back of course, like on T.V." She moved to look out the window. "Doubt I can cozy up to him and pull it out without him noticing."

"And we were doing so well. Had Miriam Patrice thinking she was losing it. I bet if she hadn't brought in these so-called relatives, she would have resigned. Once you were leading the community, I'm sure we could convince them to sell us that land and our little village would become a reality." Del smiled at the thought of his plan for condominiums, houses and definitely retail space out in the fields that grew those damn sunflowers. Why couldn't Miriam Patrice see the benefits to not only her community, but to the whole county?

"Well, dearest uncle, Miriam Patrice isn't losing it now. Enough of all this, we need to admit defeat for now. Finding Tater is my primary concern. I got him into this and can't stand the thought of him getting into trouble. I'm heading back to my room. I'll call you with any news and please call me if you hear from Tater, okay?"

Annalise moved to the door, but turned. "I love you, Uncle Del. Stay warm and cozy. I'm sure you're right. All will be well. Tater is a man of many talents." Under her breath, she added, "I sure hope so, because he's going to need all of them if that Hammond guy finds him."

She reversed her steps and climbed slowly up the staircase to her room. After locking the door, she pulled out her phone for one more call to Tater. No answer. She sank to her knees and pulled out her rosary, thinking that it wasn't right to pray for Tater, since what they did was definitely not very Christian. Her next confession would knock Father Greg out of the confessional.

CHAPTER EIGHTEEN

Dash got out of bed calling for his cousin. "Wakey, wakey, William. We have a problem."

Billy came out of his bedroom with the blankets wrapped around him. He staggered slightly, holding his stomach. "Dash, I don't think, I know we have a problem. One is, where's T.J? Do we have heat? It couldn't be that cold out that we're freezing in here, right?"

"I'm going to check the thermostat. I set it at 68 so the furnace or whatever heats this place should be chugging along. Awfully quiet." He reached for a light switch and got nothing. He started to swear, but remembered he was trying to mend his ways. Ah, fatherhood.

He moved down the stairs with Billy following, still moaning and holding his stomach.

Dash looked out the front window after scrapping some frost from the inside. He shook his head. "Not good, Billy, not good. But it looks like they have lights over at the motherhouse."

He pulled his phone out and called Jumbo. Checking the time on his phone, he hoped the ex-soldier was one of those early risers, a holdover from his military days.

Jumbo answered on the first ring. "Dash, what's up?"

"Not the temperature here, that's for sure. You guys have heat over there? I'm thinking we lost whatever heat source we had. Have you looked outside recently?"

"Yes to both your questions. It's almost toasty here and it's a damn blizzard out there. Been checking all night. We had a burp, but the generators kicked in. No electricity?"

Letting out a sigh, Dash shook his head and then remembered to reply verbally. "No, which explains the lack of heat. I'm going to check our exits to see if we might make our way over there. Check the floor plan and head over to the church. You should be able to access it without going outside. If you can open the front door that would be closest for us. Over and out."

Dash looked at Billy who still clutched his midsection.

"Listen William. I'm going to get dressed and will see about these doors and getting out of here. Sit still until you feel better, which I'm hoping is soon. If you can dress, do it in layers and pack up the rest of your stuff. If we make the move, we move hook, line and sinker."

Billy mumbled something Dash took as agreement.

Upstairs, Dash grabbed the remaining blankets from Billy's room and threw them onto Mae and T.J. He then put layer after layer on following his own advice. Even though his movement felt a bit restricted, he was warm. When finished, he looked like the old combat soldier he was.

Turning to Mae and T.J. he said, "You two stay under the covers until we're ready to move. The main house is warm so we will head there unless I can get some heat started here."

When starting the heat proved futile, he spent the next half hour trying to determine if either the front or back door would open. Since the back of the house did not take a direct hit from the wind and snow, this would be their point of exit. After searching for a shovel, he found a broom and settled for that. He broke through the icecap on the snow which measured about one foot. There were layers of ice and snow.

He walked back into the living room, ready to call Jumbo. Billy was sitting there moaning. Mae came down the stairs wrapped in a blanket.

"Since you are sitting in the dark, I can assume we are

without power." She looked at Billy. "What's wrong with you?"

"Dash, those pills you gave me aren't working. My gut is still doing flip-flops."

Turning to Dash, Mae asked, "You gave Billy some meds from my bag?"

Shaking his head, Dash replied, "Hell no, I gave him pills from my bag. The ones the Army gave me."

"How old are they? And what makes you think you can dispense medicine, Colonel? Next, you'll be performing surgery." Mae said angrily.

He glared at his wife. "Let me say if you were spilling your guts all over the floor, I could tuck them back inside and stitch you up so you could be transported back to camp. Now, Doctor, I don't suppose you thought to take a course or two in electrical engineering. Sure could use some expertise right now."

Billy groaned. "I think I'm dying."

"If you keep moaning, there will be no thinking about it. Damn but you're a whiner." Dash said to his cousin.

"That's smart coming from the guy I had to help to the toilet when you smashed your head in. Good thing I didn't have to wipe your butt."

Mae sighed loudly. "Enough!" She rummaged through her medicine bag and produced some pills. "Here, Billy, take these. Will take about a half hour, but should put you to rights. And drink plenty of water. Stay hydrated. Crawl back in bed with Thomas while I help Einstein here."

"You keep talking like that, Maevis, and you can find your own way to the motherhouse."

Under her breath, she called her husband a not so nice name.

He turned to her. "What did you say?"

"Nothing, my love," she said with a smile. "I'll help Billy back to bed. Might crawl in with him and Thomas." She started for the stairs. "Seriously, let me know what I should be doing. And, by the by, I'm feeling much better, thank you, dearest heart."

Dash looked around for something to throw at his wife's back as she scrambled up the stairs.

Talking to himself, Dash mumbled, "Walking is going to be difficult for Mae and non-existent for T.J. Have to carry him. God, I hope I don't have to carry Billy." He turned to see his three companions making their way slowly down the stairs. Layered up for sure, they could barely move their arms and legs.

T.J. walked stiff-legged over to his father. "Look Daddy, I have my underpants on over my jammies. Wait til I tell Grandpa. He's going to laugh. Can I call him now?"

"No, too early even for Grandpa. Are you warm?"

"Yes, sir."

"Well, then that's all that matters. Maevis, what about you?"

"Since I have on everything I brought, yes. What's the plan?" She said as she guided Billy to a chair.

"What about William Patrick? Is he going to make it, or should we just bury him in the snow and ice until spring?"

Billy glared at him. "Very funny. Remind me again why I think you're my best friend?"

"You don't. Everyone else does so we just go with the flow." He caught himself and asked, "Sorry, how are you doing? And no, I won't leave you behind. You have too many siblings who would take my sorry head off if I let something happen to their precious brother."

Mae wandered over to her husband. "Gentlemen, and I use that term loosely, we've been side-tracked here. Again, what's the plan, assuming you have one, oh mighty warrior?"

"Working on it now. Sit tight while Jumbo and I confer." He punched Jumbo's number into the phone.

After nodding several times, Dash rang off. "Listen up. Jumbo is bringing the Hummer over to the side of the house.

He's clearing it off now. Pack everything. We're bugging out. Be sure to check every place for everything." He looked at his son, "I'm not coming back so if Petey Rabbit is left behind, he stays behind. Got it? Start now. I'll call Jumbo when we are ready."

The scramble began. Mae helped T.J. and secured Petey Rabbit in his backpack. After the troops reported that everything was packed, Dash went through each room to make sure all was clear. He gathered the bags at the back door, muttering how the Allies brought less to invade France.

"When Jumbo gets here, I'll load the luggage. Mae, you're first. I'll help you walk, then I'll carry T.J. Billy, you're last but for me. If you don't feel up to walking on your own," he raised his hand, "say so. Swear to God, I can carry you if needed."

Dash studied his cousin's face. Billy looked about to cry.

"I can't believe how useless I've become. Pretty sure I can walk to the car. Think Mae's meds are taking hold. Sorry to be such a bother, Dash. I owe you one."

Dash waved him off. "Forget about it. Listen, I'll do a final walk-thru and close up."

Billy added, "Don't forget the water pipes. Think you're supposed to let the water drip. Would hate for the pipes to burst. Man, this is more complicated than life should be." He moved to the back of the house while Dash ran around checking all the faucets.

Arriving at the back door, Dash said, "We're off. Billy, grab a blanket so I can cover T.J.'s face. Limit the exposed skin, folks. Hoping we won't be out long but no sense taking a chance."

Operation Transfer commenced. It went much smoother than Dash anticipated. He only fell face first into the snow drift once. T.J. was brave and quiet, while Billy muttered and cursed the whole time he trudged from the house to the car. At last, Jumbo put the Hummer in gear and slowly made his way back to the motherhouse.

They hit a few bumps in the road causing Dash to comment on the state of the statuary they observed when arriving.

Turning to Billy, he said, "I suppose we can pay for any damage, or do you think Miri Pat will write it off as part of the hazards of hiring us?"

Billy sat shivering. "I don't give a flying …"

Mae slapped her hand over his mouth. "William Patrick McCafferty, don't make me call your mother."

Jumbo glanced at Dash and smiled.

The offloading went swiftly. Tiny joined them at the door. He carried Mae inside while Dash took T.J. Then Tiny pulled Billy out of the car and deposited him in the foyer. Once the Hummer was empty, the group moved to Miri Pat's office. They began the process of de-layering, draping their outer garments over the chairs.

"The head honcho is in the nether belly checking on the mechanicals. Some lady named Marie who could pass for a drill sergeant is downstairs commanding everyone around, but I'm pretty sure we'll have a hot breakfast before long," Tiny announced.

"And all's right with the world," Dash proclaimed. "Marie is one good cook. Look forward to whatever she concocts." He helped T.J. out of his boots. "We'll use this as our base camp for now. Store your things neatly." He wrapped his arms around Mae. "You doing okay? Sore?"

"I'll be fine. Sore, yes, but think moving is good. Warm would be better. I'm going to take Thomas and head downstairs. Maybe we can help." She turned to Billy who stood like an ice sculpture. "Billy, you okay? Dash, help him. Make him move."

"What's wrong with him?" asked Jumbo.

"Mild stomach upset. Too much pizza last night. I tried to give him some pills but apparently they were too old to help," Dash reported.

Billy squeaked, "Mild only if you didn't have it. Ask my stomach."

Jumbo looked at Tiny who stared back.

Catching the looks that passed between the men, Dash asked, "What? Report."

"Funny your friend should have a stomach complaint. Same thing happened to us. We spent a few hours moaning like him until that little one who was a nurse, gave us something." Jumbo said.

Billy shuffled over. "You guys were sick last night?" He turned to Dash. "We all ate the same pizza, meat-lovers. I set them set aside for us and Jumbo. Think we had food poisoning?"

Dash asked Jumbo. "Did Ilene, that's the nurse, report that any of the sisters got sick? I mean several had the pepperoni pizza. Same sausage was on the meat pizzas. If no one else got sick, it means the pizzas you ate were tampered with, just enough of something to make you sick, but not kill you. Just a thought."

Billy blanched at that thought, "Sick but not dead?"

The men stood in silence digesting this.

Changing the subject, Billy shivered as he spoke. "I'm never coming to Kentucky again. Never, ever, even in springtime, summer or fall. Never going to thaw out."

The two ex-soldiers, Dash and Jumbo, exchanged glances. Tiny just frowned.

"And that, gentlemen, is a fine example of who we do not want at our side in the mountains of Afghanistan. If he thinks this is cold …" Dash said.

"Oh right, always have to outdo the rest of us. Cold, hot, wet, dry. If you weren't my ride home, I'd say something insulting to you," Billy said with an emphatic nod.

"Oh, be quiet. We're here and it's time to put this mission to rest. Let's get some coffee and decide on the day's plan. Now move it," the colonel commanded.

As the men were leaving for the dining hall, Dash

stopped Billy, waving the others on.

"You know what this confirms, don't you?" he asked.

Billy nodded. "Yes, inside job. Someone or several someones could have planted the bugs. And one could have easily gotten back into the guest house to steal Petey Rabbit. And one could have donned the gorilla mask to scare Mae. Here's the rub, dear cousin, I'm pretty sure all the staff had left yesterday after cleaning up the luncheon stuff. None were around to tamper with the pizzas – at least that's what I remember."

"Let's talk to Ilene and Irma. See if anyone else were in the slightest way sick. With any luck, our duo was able to pick up some inside gossip. Women are just slightly worse than men when chit-chatting about things."

"You're right. Innocent until proven guilty, or so I'm told," said the counselor as he headed down the hall.

"Listen, I'm going to find Miri Pat to make sure all is well. You find Mae and bring her up to date with our thinking. If Ilene or Irma are around, use your charm to get some answers. I'll join you in a few."

Billy laughed. "Don't think I have that much charm, but will do what I can. Tell Sis I said good morning."

The dining hall bustled. Marie had commandeered the kitchen. She directed Irma to crack eggs for scrambling. Bacon and sausage were sizzling on the stove. On a frigid day, Marie's solution for happiness was a warm hearty breakfast.

The sisters were helping themselves to the little boxes of dry cereal, their usual fare. Mae got a box for Thomas and settled him at a table. Introduction were made and T.J. discovered Sister Joseph Thomas. They immediately bonded, since T.J. said they both had the same name, being reversed didn't matter to the four-year old.

Mae left the little one chattering away about the adventure here at the North Pole. He told the sisters how his Uncle Sammy liked to dress up as Santa Claus, but you couldn't say anything, or you'd hurt his feelings. "I know it's him because he has the same crinkles around his eyes as Uncle Sammy and wears the same perfume." Shrugging he declared, "Presents, from Santa Claus or Uncle Sammy are good."

Dash found the mechanicals room behind the laundry at the other end of the basement. He knocked on the door before pushing it open.

Sister Miriam Patrice, dressed in jeans and a sweatshirt, stood looking at the gauges. She was talking to someone on her phone. She turned to Dash and motioned for him to join her. After telling the man she was speaking with to 'please hold,' she said to Dash, "I'm on with Dowd. He can't make it in. Not only are the roads not plowed yet, but there was an accident on the main road into town. This is blocking the road. I told him to stay home."

Dash nodded. "May I ask if you are making notes of what he's telling you, in case something goes wrong?"

Miri Pat handed the phone to Dash. "Here, you talk to him. He can assure you that I may not be a certified whatever, but he has taught me the way around some of these machines."

Laughing, Dash took the phone. After being reassured Miri Pat knew what she was doing, sort of, he asked Dowd about the workers who had recently been in and around the campus. The conversation ended with Dowd saying he would collect his records for the last several months and call back.

"Well, Miri Pat, have you had breakfast yet? Let's walk and talk. I have much speculation to run by you. And you need to know, your brother is recovering from a bad bit of pizza."

Miri Pat stopped. Looking directly into Dash's eyes, she said, "The undertones aren't good. I assume Billy is fine, or you would have led with that. 'Bad pizza.' Are you saying that some of my lot, as you call them, also got sick? Haven't had any reports."

"Don't know about the others and their reaction to the pizza, just yet. William is checking on that. Let's eat before we discuss what needs to be discussed. I, for one, am starving."

"I hope you're ready for those little boxes of cereal we had as kids. That is our usual breakfast for most of the sisters. Gives the kitchen staff … Oh no, I bet none of our people will make it in."

"Have someone call them, so they don't try. Good old Marie has taken charge of the kitchen, or so I'm told. All will be well unless your larder is empty. I've seen that woman make a ten-course meal out of nothing. Talk about loaves and fishes being multiplied. And, if worst comes to worst, Tiny, Jumbo and I will forage for provisions."

"Lead on, MacDuff," said Miri Pat.

Dash and Miri Pat stopped at the entrance to the dining hall. The sisters were indeed chowing down and talking about the weather. The aroma of bacon, ham, eggs, and hot rolls filled the room.

Dash took a deep breath and murmured a prayer of thanks for Marie deciding to come along.

He spotted T.J. moving from table to table showing off his underpants over his jammies. The sisters laughed appropriately and the little one went on to regale them with the tale of moving out of the guest house.

Miri Pat leaned over to Dash. "He's really a chip off the old block. I remember you entertaining the neighborhood with your antics. Actually, you and Billy did a good imitation of Bob Hope and Bing Crosby with Mae as Dorothy Lamour. Wish someone had thought to tape those performances."

"I don't remember any of that."

"All impromptu. You guys cracked my dad up. One of my fondest memories is of him retelling your entertainment. Your dad wasn't so amused. A bit too serious is Owen."

"Remember he's not Irish, so he has no real soul, or so

my mother often told him. Lord, you Irish are often unbearable," Dash said.

"Only to those with no soul. And how dare you speak of the Irish like that! If ever there was an Irish Hammond, dear sir, it is you. Rotten to the core."

Dash shook his head, trying to deny her pronouncement, as he guided her to the table where her brother, Mae and the two security men were feasting on hot food.

Billy nodded to them. "If you want more than cereal, head to the kitchen. Marie is taking special requests. She made toast and sweet tea for me. Told me it would settle my stomach. I'm about to fall asleep at the wheel here. After this I'm finding a corner to nap in." He motioned to Jumbo. "Where did you put the mattresses you brought down for last night?"

Jumbo blushed. "You ain't gonna like this but we dragged them into the men's room. To be close to the toilet, just in case."

"Like it or not, I'm going to sleep wherever they may be. That's how drained I am," Billy said.

Miri Pat laughed. "Oh, ye of the temperamental constitution. I'd tell you to be more like Dash, but you'd only scoff, so I'm telling you to be more like Mae. Now there's a woman who can hold her own in this world."

Mae nodded. "Thank you. Words to warm my heart."

Dash rolled his eyes and shook his head. "Eat up so we can get started on ending all this."

CHAPTER NINETEEN

After the meal, Dash and Billy headed over to the church to investigate the tap-tap sound. As Dash rounded the corner, he stopped short almost running into a man. Billy then bumped into Dash. A bit of a chain reaction.

"Look where you're going, why don't you?" the man said angrily.

"Like I can see around corners." Dash took a step back. "Who are you and what are you doing here?"

"I can ask you the same questions. Haven't seen you around here before. Why don't you go first?" The stranger said, holding a basket covered with a kitchen towel.

Dash leaned back against the wall to better study this new player, trying not to appear cautious but casual. Six three or six four. Longish blond hair tied back, a beard. The man cradled the basket with his arms across his chest, mimicking Dash, and stared back at him.

The tension was beginning to mount.

"How did you get in the building?" Dash asked.

The man held up a key. "No breaking and entering, if that's what you think."

"And how did you get here to Marianwood? Last time we checked, the roads were impassible."

"Didn't take the roads. I came by horse."

"By horse?"

Billy muttered, "A bit of an echo in here. And far be it

from me to break up this scintillating conversation but let me introduce myself. William McCafferty, my sister is Miriam Patrice, head of this place." He held out his hand.

The intruder, in Dash's mind, did not offer his hand nor his name, but held the basket close.

"Let's start again. Who the hell are you, and what are you doing here?" Dash asked again, this time with all the authority of a combat veteran.

The man looked from Dash to Billy and back. He rubbed his hand on his pants and shook Billy's hand. "Vincent Oliver, or Ollie as I'm known. I work here, mind the chickens. Figured no one would remember to feed them. To check on them." He shifted the basket. "Oh, maybe that's where you were heading."

"Chickens?" Dash asked. "Damn, forgot all about them."

"Ah the echo is back. Chickens you say," Billy said. He nodded to Dash. "And you want to raise them back home. Wait til Mae hears this."

After scowling, Dash put out his hand. "Dash Hammond, cousin to Sister Miriam Patrice. Sorry."

Oliver didn't shake the offered hand, but started walking down the hall toward the dining hall. "Didn't see any cars from the cooking staff. Talked with Dowd earlier and he said he couldn't make it out of his street. Figured someone should check on the hens. I live on the other side of the sunflower meadow, so I hopped on Zeus, that's the horse, and made my way over here."

Dash almost grabbed the man's arm but stopped. "Hey, where is this chicken coop? You have a key to the outbuildings?"

"The winter coop is inside the old dairy barn. Move them inside for the winter. And yes, I have a key to it and a key to the door I came in. Any more questions? Because I'd kill for a hot cup of coffee and a bite to eat. One of those little boxes of cereal sounds good right now."

"You are in for a treat. My sister-in-law is cooking up a storm. She'll appreciate a hearty appetite." Dash said as he fell in step with the man. He pointed to the basket. "Would I be wrong in assuming you have fresh eggs there?"

Ollie grinned. "Can't get any fresher than this. Small yield this morning. Think the storm last night upset them. Hens, like women, get a bit touchy about the smallest thing."

Billy laughed. "Yeah, like ten feet of snow, howling winds and ice raining down causing a real racket."

The three men entered the dining hall. All nodded as they passed the sisters who were relaxing after their meals.

Ollie obviously knew where to take the eggs, heading straight for the kitchen. Dash and Billy followed.

Marie thanked Ollie more vociferously than necessary, or so thought her brother-in-law. He watched her eyes light up at this new specimen of masculinity. Good thing Sheriff Sam stayed home. His brother wouldn't understand Marie's appreciation of the chicken farmer.

"Gentlemen, scrambled eggs, hot oatmeal, and some fried ham await you," Marie said, then added in her softest mother tone, "You might want to wash up before you eat. I bet you know where the bathrooms are."

Ollie dipped his head slightly. "Yes, I do, and I am very thankful for your kind invitation to partake of your hot meal. Is there coffee around?"

Dash rolled his eyes at Billy who just smiled while he mouthed 'partake.'

Ollie went off to wash up and then filled up a plate. He sat by himself.

Dash loaded up a second plate of food, causing Billy to comment on the amount of food his cousin was consuming.

Billy said, "How can you eat so much? I can barely look at food."

"I'm a growing boy and I had enough sense not to eat the pizza last night."

"Growing your waistband for sure. Remember we're

not as young as we used to be. It takes longer to work off those calories, my friend."

Dash snorted. He was going to join Ollie until he saw the look on his wife's face.

Dismayed, Dash watched Mae ogle the newcomer. When he sat down at her table, she leaned into her husband. "Who is that and where did you find him?"

"Put those green eyes back into their sockets, woman." He held up his left hand, wiggling the third finger. "You're married in case you've forgotten."

"Married but not dead. My, my, but he is gorgeous."

Dash scoffed, "He hasn't got anything I don't have."

Mae's smile broadened. "Yes, but his is younger."

"Ouch!"

"I go for younger men. I married you after all, didn't I?" Mae asked.

Throwing down his fork, Dash turned to her. "For God's sake, Mae, I'm twenty-six days younger than you, not the twenty-six years you have on Ollie. Old enough to be his mother." Under his breath, he whispered, "You dirty old lady."

Billy jumped in, "Mae, he's a chicken farmer and rode his horse over here to make sure the chickens were fed and warm. Not something your husband thought to check, but then again with his advanced age it most probably slipped his mind. It's all that food he's eating; taking away brain power to digest it all."

Mae's eyes opened wider. "A horse. This just gets better." She winked at Dash. "Bet he's a very good rider."

Dash looked up to see Ollie approaching. Under his breath he said to Mae, "Behave, or I swear I will lock you up."

Standing, Dash made the introduction.

Ollie nodded politely but turned to Dash. "Do you want to see the chickens and my horse? Make sure I'm legit."

Before Mae could say that she would be happy to come, Dash answered in the affirmative. "Be glad to. Billy, do you want to join us?"

"Hell, no. Go outside again? No, I'm happy to sit here and sip my tea."

At that moment, T.J. ran up to his father. "Daddy, can we build a snowman? Mommy, you want to come?"

Dash answered for her. "Unfortunately, Mommy has work to do here with Uncle Billy. But let's put on another layer or two and we'll see about that snowman, right after we visit some chickens and a horse."

"Can I ride the horse? Can I, Daddy?"

Mae answered. "No, no, you may not. You don't have a helmet, and I can't trust your father to stand by your side."

"Ma'am, I'll make sure the little tyke is safe. He can sit on Zeus. We won't walk around. No harm," Ollie said with a smile and a slight dip of his head.

Mae flashed him her best smile and whispered to Dash, "Zeus for Adonis."

Dash hurriedly guided Ollie and T.J. out of the dining hall.

The visit to the barn didn't take as long as Dash envisioned. The chicken coop was impressive, as was Ollie's knowledge of the birds. And Zeus was one imposing horse. Massive is how Dash would describe him but as gentle as a little bunny.

T.J.'s eyes grew wide when he approached the animal. Ollie held the reins and guided T.J. so he could pet the horse. Then he hoisted the child onto the steed. Dash immediately went to the opposite side just in case T.J. started to slip. True to his word, Ollie didn't let Zeus take a step.

Dash snapped photos so Grandpa and Father Tom could see the brave little boy.

Father and son thanked Ollie, who said he was off to snowplow around the motherhouse. He asked where Dash parked his car and said he would clear the area for whenever the northerners wanted to leave so they would have smooth driving.

Dash and T.J. made the world's smallest snowman before they decided it was indeed too cold to be mucking about. After more photos were taken, the duo headed indoors to warm up.

Checking in on the crew, Dash learned that Tiny and Jumbo were doing a perimeter check even though they were certain no one in their right mind would be out. Dash remarked that whoever was doing this wasn't quite right in the mind, as they put it.

Their next assignment was to scour the church for whatever apparatus was making the tap-tap-tap sound. Sister Bernadette agreed to talk with them about what she heard and where she heard it.

CHAPTER TWENTY

Back in the office, Dash, Mae, Billy and Miri Pat sat around the table. The overall consensus was that whoever was pulling these pranks, to put it mildly, had not thought this through.

"And that's it in a nutshell, Miri," Billy said. "We think one of your lay staff and possibly one of your own is behind all this, but don't know why."

"So open up, dearest Sister," Dash said. "What have you, you and the board, been up to that would upset someone outside the community? Selling off more land, which I understand is under consideration, but how would that affect outsiders? I would think more jobs would be one of the results, and nowadays, who could object to that? Thoughts?"

Miri Pat leaned back in her chair. "Unbelievable. No, no, it can't be one of our staff. They are the kindest people, always going out of the way to take care of us. And to accuse my sisters, unthinkable."

She rose, walking to the window where she stood, hands in her pockets. The mood in the room was tense as the trio watched her body tighten with each deep breath she took. After a few minutes, she turned to them, scowling. With all the authority she could muster, she announced, "You're dismissed. You can go home now. I will handle this. Thank you for coming." She returned to staring out the window.

The trio looked at each other, stunned. Billy slowly shook his head. Mae squirmed in her seat, about to rise, when

Dash signaled for her to stay. He walked over to Miri Pat, standing so close he definitely invaded her personal space. He watched her inhale deeply.

"Miri, when I was ten I didn't take that tone of voice from the principal at St. Mary's, so don't be offended when I say: bullshit. I didn't come all this way to be sent home. My son has been upset, my wife assaulted, your brother and my team poisoned. If you think that commanding tone is going to send me packing, you, dear cousin, have a few more lessons to learn about this incorrigible old soldier."

He turned her around. "So, get out that rosary and head over to church. Get on your knees and start praying because all hell is about to break lose. You want me gone? Fine, I'll go but only when I can drag the miscreant or miscreants out with me."

Miri's face seethed with rage. She glared at Billy and Mae, then pushed past Dash to exit the room.

Billy sighed. "Thanks for riling her up. Just because she's a sister doesn't mean she doesn't have the temper of a red-headed Irish wench. Remember she is a McCafferty."

He sighed again. "I suppose I should go after her and apologize for your behavior. You didn't mean it, did you, that we have to stay until you uncover the culprit?" Billy said. "I'm about to drop. How cowardly is it if I take a nap before I cross paths with Miri? She can be fierce, you know."

His words fell on Dash's deaf ears. He stared out the window, his stance tense.

Mae reached over to Billy. "Find a quiet spot and rest. I'll find Thomas. He's with Marie helping prepare the lunch. I'll think about what to do with Miri Pat and ..." She nodded towards her husband.

They left the room but not before Mae said, "Like Schwarzenegger I'll be back, and we will have words. Think on your sins."

Rather than think, he acted. Calling Tiny and Jumbo, he arranged a meeting in one of the second-floor rooms. Then he summoned Irma and Ilene. Told to drop everything and meet upstairs, they agreed.

Dash laid out his theory to them. "Now, I need to figure out just who is behind this. I almost don't care why at this point. So ladies, what did you observe last night while the pizza was being passed around?"

"In other words, since no lay staff was present, which sister do I think could have dosed the pizza, not proven but surmised, if that's it?" asked Irma.

"In a nutshell," Dash answered.

She glanced at Ilene and then they both stared at the ground, deep in thought.

The men sat silently.

"It's the younger one, Sister Anna something. Didn't catch her name properly. She flitted around. Volunteered to help Billy, so she took those pizzas back to the kitchen. Problem, Dash, is this: if she added something to cause distress, where did she get it? Did she know these guys were coming, and were they the target, or was it you and Billy?" Irma asked. "You don't think she carries around drugs in her pocket, do you?"

Ilene spoke next. "It wouldn't take much planning. There are any number of over-the-counter items that could cause this type of distress. Once she heard about the pizza dinner, she could have gone to her room for some pills and crushed them. With all the spices, it would be barely noticeable I should think. Bigger question is why."

"Should be simple enough. Ask the C.O. of the outfit. She's bound to know. Ain't this Anna something her second in command?" Jumbo said.

Dash moved his mouth around. "Slight problem there." And he told them what transpired before they met.

Irma started laughing. "That's my colonel. Now we know why you were never in the diplomatic corps. So what do we do now, since packing our bags is out of the question? I mean even if we wanted to leave, the weather is against us. Does anyone know the forecast? Are we here until spring?"

"According to the latest weather report, all this will start melting tomorrow. Figure we have twenty-four hours before this Miri can call the police to escort us off the property," Jumbo reported.

"That's not going to happen. She'll see I'm right and apologize for being, well, whatever you want to call it. Impolite doesn't quite cover it. We drag our bodies down here to help her, and she is as ungrateful as it gets," Dash said.

"I say we find this Anna something and beat the truth out of her. Sound like a plan?" said Tiny.

The rest looked at him, saying collectively and emphatically, "No!"

Dash stood. "The first part, finding Sister Annalise, is where we start. No beating though. Let's hear her side before we judge her. Let's split up, as they say in the movies. Phones on. Report in if you spot her; don't approach until I get there. Let's roll."

CHAPTER TWENTY-ONE

T.J., backpack tucked at his feet, watched as his mother and his Auntie Re rushed around the kitchen to make lunch for everyone. Tired of all the noise, he picked up the backpack heavy with books and sketch pads and pencils and, of course, Petey Rabbit.

"Mommy, I'm going to find a quiet place to read, okay?" he asked.

"Yes, sweetie, try to stay out of the way so you don't get run over. Love you," Mae said with a smile.

T.J. knew just the place for reading and drawing. He walked up the stairs and down the hall to the Reading Room, the place with the beautiful windows. He turned the doorknob and entered the room. The sun had come out, and once again the room shone with brilliant colors streaming from the stained-glass windows.

All alone, he now had time to study each window and make a sketch to show his grandpa. He walked past each window just to get another glimpse at them.

The first window depicted a young girl with a puppy in a garden of books. In the next window the girl was older, seated beneath a tree, reading. Again, the puppy was by her side. The window at the center of the back wall was similar to the insert in the door to the Reading Room. A tree with books on the branches instead of leaves filled the space. No girl, no puppy.

In the next window, the girl wore a long blue skirt and a straw hat. Her dog had grown as well and sat obediently next to her as she gazed off into a field where a man was working. She shielded her eyes from the sun with a book.

The final window made T.J. very sad since the woman sat next to a tombstone, leaning on it. There was a name on it, but T.J. couldn't make it out. The dog lay by her side, his paws resting on a book. Although the sun was shining in the window, the overall effect was one of great sadness and loss.

"Poor Miss Victoria," T.J. said aloud.

He pushed a small table over to the first window and pulled out his pad and colored pencils, aligning them neatly. He glanced up at the window and began to sketch it.

Deep in concentration, he jumped when he felt a slight touch on his shoulder. He turned, expecting to see his daddy or mommy surprising him, but the surprise was the woman from the windows.

"Oh, I'm sorry. I didn't mean to startle you. Just wanted to see your picture. You're a good artist, young man," the woman said.

T.J. tilted his head to study her. "Are you Miss Victoria, the ghost from the cemetery? You look just like her." He pointed to the window where the woman gazed at the field. "You still have that dress on. Where's your dog?"

"Oh, poor Lady. She passed on a long time ago. I wish she could be a ghost with me. I could use the company. It's a lonely business being a ghost, as you call me. I prefer the word 'spirit.' It's not as scary as 'ghost,' don't you think? And you're not scared, are you?"

After giving it some thought, T.J. answered, "I'm a Hammond. We're soldiers, so it's hard to scare us." He screwed up his mouth. "I guess you might be right about 'ghost' and 'spirit.' If you yell 'spirit,' I doubt the kids on the playground would run; but yell 'ghost,' and everyone would scatter."

He wrinkled his brow and then asked, "I don't suppose

you know Ned Parker from St. Mary's School in Clover Pointe? He's an expert on ghosts and goblins. Very smart kid."

Miss Victoria shook her head, then pulled a chair over and sat down to lean over his drawing.

"I really enjoyed making sketches for these windows. Do you like them? I wanted to tell my story. Can you understand them?"

"A little bit. You liked to read even when you were a little girl. And you love your dog. I have a dog. Her name is Pansy Pup. She has floppy ears and loves to run with me." He leaned over to Miss Victoria. "Sometimes she has an accident on the floor, and I clean it up before my daddy sees. He doesn't like when that happens."

Victoria's eyes widen. "Oh dear, is your daddy a mean man? He won't get rid of your puppy, will he? My father was very mean to me. He took my kitten away and always threatened to banish Lady to the stables. She wouldn't have liked that at all."

T.J. held up his hand and shook his head. "No, no, my daddy is my best friend. He has a dog named Charlie who guards us and also helps Daddy when he feels low. Sometimes we all curl up on the living room floor and tell funny stories."

He studied his new spirit friend. "Why do the trees and plants have books instead of leaves and flowers? That's not how it works."

Victoria smiled at him. "Well, maybe not, but books were the only friends I had and when I read, I felt like I was blossoming like a flower. Does that make sense? I wrote something like that in one of my notebooks, but I'm not sure anyone ever read them to learn just what I meant." She glanced around the room. "But they are pretty, aren't they? They make me glad to see all the bright colors."

"Most of them are happy ones, but the last one is very sad. Is that supposed to be the grave of your boyfriend? Did your daddy really kill him?" T.J. asked as politely as he could, thinking this might be one of those things grownups said you shouldn't talk about.

The spirit got up and crossed the room to gaze at the last window. "This isn't Hamish's grave. My daddy never said where he buried him. He didn't want me grieving at his grave and always taking flowers there. Like I said, my daddy was a mean man."

"Is that why you keep searching for his grave, I mean your boyfriend's, not your daddy's?" T.J. moved to her side. "Sister Agnes Marie said you search the cemetery every time there is a full moon."

Victoria smiled down at the little boy. "I'm afraid all those stories are not true. Everyone thought it was more romantic if I searched for Hamish, but I do know a fresh grave when I see one and there were no new graves, so my daddy lied to me. He didn't bury him in the cemetery. I don't know where."

"Have you thought of the lake? Lots of people bury people in a lake. You never see them again," T.J. reported, then he thought about his daddy and grimaced. Could he be wrong, and his daddy never said that about the lake?

Victoria returned her gaze to the window. "Can you keep a secret?"

T.J. nodded. "I'm good at keeping secrets. Just ask my grandpa."

She leaned down to look him in the eye. "My daddy hid all my mama's jewels, even the pearl necklace. He didn't want me to have them, even though Mama told me they were mine. I don't want everyone looking for them, tearing up the house and the garden. I searched and searched in the house. The jewels aren't there, but they might be in the cemetery." She reached for his hand. "Don't tell, please."

Taking her hand in his, T.J. said, "You can count on me, Miss Victoria." He drew a line across his lips, now sealed.

They walked around the room, studying each window.

Victoria told why she chose the colors and how she worked with the craftsmen to make the windows. By the time they finished, T.J. was laughing at the funny stories she told about her puppy Lady.

"I bet you're glad your daddy didn't take her away. He wasn't a very good daddy, was he?"

"No, he wasn't. But I got him in the end. He didn't want me to inherit the farm and house. He wanted a horrible cousin to come up from Georgia and take over. But I tricked everyone. I practiced and practiced until I could imitate his handwriting. Then I wrote out a will leaving everything to me," she smiled and winked. "I tore up the one my daddy wrote. What do you think of that?"

Clapping his hands, T.J. said, "My daddy would say, 'Way to go, Miss Victoria.' He doesn't like mean people."

"Was it your father who tried to catch me the other night?"

"Yes, he was very confused when he saw your footprints. Ghosts don't leave footprints, do they?"

She winked. 'I wanted to trick him since he nearly caught me. I couldn't have that, could I?"

T.J. rubbed his eyes. "Miss Victoria, I'm tired. I couldn't sleep a wink last night. Did you hear the wind howling and the ice hitting the windows? I think I'm going to put my head down for a minute. Is that okay?"

Victoria patted his head. "Please get your sleep. I'll visit with you again, okay? Remember to keep my secret."

T.J. closed his eyes and fell asleep in minutes.

Mae opened the door to find her son sound asleep. Instead of castigating him for wandering off, she tiptoed to the table and joined him. Soon mother and son were napping.

CHAPTER TWENTY-TWO

Billy grabbed a blanket from the pile in the corner of the office and crossed the hall to the drawing room. If memory served him, there was a very comfortable sofa which should fit him.

He climbed on it and wrapped himself tightly in the blanket. Sighing deeply, he closed his eyes and was fast asleep before he could worry about anything.

An hour or so later, he sat straight up, asking himself, what the devil was that noise? Trying to stretch his back, he glanced at his watch. Time sure flies when you don't want it to.

Damn. The banging persisted.

Billy stood looking for the source of the noise. Across the room at the window, he saw what could only be called a black blob banging on the glass. He crossed to get a better look while he pulled out his phone. Backup. Billy was in no mood to deal with whatever or whoever was causing this racket.

Suddenly the blob disappeared. Billy peered over the edge of the window and saw a heap of black on the ground.

"Dash, drawing room asap," he said into his phone.

He tried to open the window, but it was frozen shut. Not wanting to break the glass, he picked up a cushion and used that to soften the blow as he pounded on the handle. Two pounds, try the handle. He heard a door open, turning slightly he yelled, "Over here, Dash. Someone is outside on the ground now but was banging on the window. Woke me up."

Dash pushed his cousin aside to glance down. He then whacked the lock. A few thumps later, the latch turned. He pushed and pulled at the screen until he detached it. Throwing it aside, he began to work on the storm window. When he couldn't jimmy it, he kicked a good-sized hole in it. Then he proceeded to break the glass so he could crawl through.

"Call Jumbo and Tiny. Better add Mae. Get them up here pronto."

Dash launched himself from the sill so he would clear the pile and any glass. He landed on the other side of it, face first in the deep snow and ice. Turning the mass over, he found a man under a heavy woolen coat. He squatted down, quickly checking to see if the man was alive. Then he maneuvered the body until he could hoist it onto his shoulders.

The window was large enough for one man, but not two.

"See if you can pull him off my shoulders. Get him inside and then I'll climb back through."

Billy grabbed at the body just as Tiny and Jumbo rinto the room. They immediately pushed him aside and lifted the body off Dash's shoulders.

"Get that blanket, and put him on it," Dash said.

Once inside, he turned to relatch the window and realized he would need to board the outside, since he destroyed the storm window. Not his brightest move.

Tiny immediately removed the man's coat and clothes, tossing them aside. The man had no gloves or hat or shoes.

Dash asked, "Has anyone called Mae? Ilene? We need professional medical advice. This guy is almost frozen solid." Then he voiced the question on everyone's mind. "What the hell was he doing out there, and how long was he there?"

"Where the hell is Mae? And Ilene. I've called for them." Billy asked.

"My mind just went blank. What do you do for frostbite?" Dash said.

Tiny answered, "Don't rub. Get him warm, a bath of warm water. Are you sure he's not dead?"

"Pretty sure, but he's damn cold."

The door opened. Mae rushed in, wiping her eyes.

"What's going on?" Mae asked as she looked at the man. "Was he outside?" She glanced at the window and turned to her husband, "Your handiwork?"

"Is he alive?" Dash asked. He studied his wife's face. She'd been asleep. The creases on her face and the small dots of sleep in the corner of her eyes gave her away. He smiled.

Mae bent over the patient. She drew in a deep breath. Turning to her husband, she said, "Not dead, or even close. He's drunk; reeks of it. We need to warm him up." She looked around. "Gentlemen, put a mattress on the table in the office, and then move him. It'll be easier to work there rather than bending over him. We need bowls of warm water to soak his hands and feet. Towels, lots of them. Dash, grab as many dry blankets as you can find."

Billy rushed to the office, clearing the table and moving a mattress onto it. Tiny carried the man and laid him on the table.

Irma and Ilene rushed in. They surveyed the situation. "What do you need?"

Mae answered, "Blankets, towels, bowls of warm water."

The Tydie sisters rushed back to get the necessities, shouting over their shoulders that they would find Sister Regina, the in-house nurse.

Mae took a good look at her husband. "You should get out of those wet clothes yourself. Feet?"

"Dry. These Army boots are amazing. I'll get you a pair one of these days."

"Stop talking and into dry clothes. Double-time."

She turned her attention to the patient. Wondering aloud, she asked, "Just who are you, and what the devil were you doing out in this weather?"

Jumbo asked, "Think he was out there all night? Can you tell?" He carried in the man's clothes and dropped them on the floor. He began to search the pockets.

Mae shook her head. "No, not out in the open. With the wind and temperatures last night, he would be frozen in spite of the alcohol consumed. Actually, that didn't help things."

"He must have had decent shelter; he's cold, but not frozen," Tiny added.

"Where's Miri Pat? She needs to know about this. Maybe she'll know who he is." Dash said.

"Still praying, I imagine. Billy, why don't you check the church? And get Thomas. He's asleep in the Reading Room. Take him with you. He can soothe ruffled feathers," Mae said.

Marie came in, pushing a café cart loaded with bowls of warm water. Irma and Ilene arrived with arms full of towels and blankets. Sister Regina pushed a cart loaded with medical supplies while another sister followed with a pot of tea and one of coffee.

Dash was in the corner, stripping out of his wet jeans and shirt.

"Hey Dash, give us some warning. A nearly naked man wasn't what I expected," Marie shouted.

"Hey yourself, dear sister-in-law, you've seen one Hammond, you've seen all of us. For God's sake, Marie, I'm barely naked, not nearly naked. Still got my long underwear on. Warm as toast." he said as he buttoned his shirt.

Just as Dash was pulling up a pair of dry camouflage pants, the door opened and in walked Sister Miriam Patrice in full habit, steam still coming from her ears.

"Just what is going on here?" She looked at the table and then at Dash. "Did you shoot him?"

"Look a little closer. Do you see a bullet hole? No, Miri,

I saved his life, which is why you find me putting on dry pants. Got soaked in the frozen tundra." He looked her up and down. "I see you've put on your uniform; fighting fit, are you? By the by, recognize him?"

Miri walked over to the table studying the man's face. She stepped back. "No, no, I don't."

Dash smiled as he approached the table. Tilting his head, he said, "Liar, liar, your habit's on fire."

"I thought I told you to get out of here. Go home. You're not wanted."

"And I told you to start praying. Which commandment is 'thou shalt not lie to cover up for someone and piss off an old friend who only is trying to help'?" Dash asked.

Billy who was standing by the door, T.J. in hand, answered. "Not sure there is one that covers that whole scenario. Obviously, God didn't plan for all contingencies. How's the guy doing?"

Miri Pat got into Dash's face. "I still want you out of here. Now."

Dash looked down at her. He moved his face around, about to say something when Mae stepped forward, a warning look in her eyes.

Scowling, he said to Miri Pat, "Better women than you have told me to get out. Didn't work then, doesn't work now. Time for you to decide whose side you're on. I won't stand for this crap much longer." His eyes narrowed as he opened his mouth to add to his statement.

"Don't say it. Don't say it or I'll cut your tongue out. Swear to God. She's a sister and an old friend. Be the gentleman you're supposed to be," Mae said. "And don't think I'll forget about the women who told you to leave but you refused. Again, think on your sins, hubby dearest."

They were all distracted when the man on the table began to moan.

Mae rushed to his side, urging him to stay still.

"Why don't all of you step outside, so he doesn't panic

when he sees your anxious faces?" Mae said.

"William, stay behind in case he gets a bit crazy. We'll be right outside the door. Come, ladies and gentlemen," Dash said as he grabbed a dry sweatshirt and his son's hand.

The group stepped across the hall into the drawing room. Miri Pat moved to the broken window. She turned to Dash. "You didn't think to use the door down the hall? Some strategist you are."

Before Dash could reply, Marie announced she would be in the kitchen if needed. T.J. tugged at his daddy's hand and asked if he could return to the reading room. Dash nodded yes.

Tiny and Jumbo stood with Dash waiting for orders.

Dash watched Miri Pat and then walked over to her.

They looked at each other and both began to speak at the same time. "I'm sorry…"

"You go first, Miri. Then I'll apologize."

"I'm sorry Dash. I shouldn't have told you to get out of here."

"Ah, that's okay. As I said you're not the first woman who's said that to me. I'm sorry to have provoked you so."

A smile tickled Miri's mouth. "Just what were you going to say in there, before Mae stepped up?"

"Well, it wasn't what she thought. I wanted to say that I love you and that's why I won't leave until I know you're safe. You, and that motley McCafferty crew, were a very important part of my life as a child and still are right up until today. Don't think I ever properly thanked you for caring for that rag-tag kid from next door," Dash said.

Miri leaned into Dash. "Those were the days. We thought we had problems back then and here we are. Bigger problems to solve." She took a deep breath. "I wasn't entirely truthful with you about that man."

Dash feigned a surprise look, so Miri punched his arm.

"I don't know his name, but I've seen him around here, mainly in church. I tend to notice the lay people who attend our Masses. Ask some of the others; I'm sure they'll know. I tend to have a lot on my mind, especially of late. Does that help?"

Shrugging, Dash said, "Not much but again, it's a start. Excuse me." He walked over to Tiny and Jumbo.

"Gentlemen, Miri admits that the man has been to church here and possibly around the premises as well. We need to determine who he is and why he is here."

Jumbo added, "And what the hell was he doing outside on a day like this?"

"I'm thinking we can follow his footsteps to see where he was hiding, must be some kind of shelter out there. I'll crawl through the window," Tiny said. "That okay, Dash?"

Miri Pat stepped into the conversation. "Might I suggest that rather than climbing through the window, you exit at the end of the building? The other one can spot the tracks from an upstairs window. Again, check the map of the grounds so you're not floundering around in that freezing weather."

Dash nodded. "Okay, sounds like a better plan. Be sure you take your phone…"

He was cut off by Billy opening the door.

"He's awake, but playing like he doesn't know where he is or who he is," Billy reported. "Since I've seen the real thing after your accident, I'm not buying it but also not pushing it. Mae wants him to rest. We moved him off the table, so he doesn't fall. I've asked Ilene to remain behind to care for him until you decide what to do."

"Good. Add Irma to the mix in case he tries to do a runner. She's good in a crunch," Dash said.

Jumbo snorted. "With those feet and no shoes, he isn't crazy enough to try to escape outdoors again. Gorilla man he may be, but he'll need more than a mask to hit that cold snow."

"But we don't know he's the gorilla man. And if he is, he knows his way around this building," Tiny added. "We weren't able to find him before so we might not be able to find him again."

Billy glared at him. "Just what we need. An optimist. How'd you make it through the wars?"

"Easy, didn't enlist. Was too big, anyway. I played ball at Northern Michigan, then did some pro wrestling. Different types of war."

"How's Miri doing?" Billy asked Dash as he watched his sister stare out the window.

"Okay, better when we solve this. We did make pretty, apologizing to each other. That, and she knows when she is outgunned and outnumbered. Let's put this puppy to bed so we can all go home to our own warm comfortable beds."

The men nodded and set off on their tasks.

CHAPTER TWENTY-THREE

Dash went looking for T.J. He grimaced when he thought of how he had sent his four-year-old son off on his own. In his mind he could hear Mae giving him hell: It's not as if we have six or seven children so one is expendable. He stopped in his tracks. Wait a minute. Who left the kid on his own in the Reading Room? Ha, ammunition if needed in the parental wars. She might be smarter than him, but he was cagier.

He slowly pushed the door. T. J. sat at a table, sketch pad and pencils in front of him, hard at work on another sketch.

"Hey, little one, how are you doing? Sorry I sent you away. You shouldn't be on your own."

"I'm not." T.J. pointed to the window. "Miss Victoria is here with me. She won't let anyone hurt me. And isn't that man on the table the gorilla man? No more danger, Daddy."

"Ah, but that were true, little man. We don't know for certain he is the gorilla man and, this is important, whether he was acting alone. Remember to consider all sides before settling on a decision." Dash looked around. "Wasn't the door locked when you got here this morning? Pretty sure Tiny and Jumbo said the place, inside and out, was locked up tight." Scowling, he added, "I'll have to have a word with them."

"Daddy, the door was unlocked when I got here, so I came in. I was hoping maybe Joey T. would be here. She told me she likes to read."

Dash nodded, wondering who Joey T. was but the imagination of a four-year-old could run wild. "Would you want me to take pictures of the windows to show Gramps? I'm sure he'll love your sketches."

Putting down his pencil, T.J. asked, "Do you think we could do this for the window in my room? Would make the place very pretty, don't you think?"

"Pretty, yes. How to do it, well, we'll have to get some books on stained-glass."

"That's not hard since we own a bookstore, is it, Daddy? And we already have some of those small windows in the family room that have pictures in them. This will be fun. I'll make Miss Victoria proud of me and my windows." T.J. smiled up at his dad.

The door opened and Sister Joseph Thomas walked in.

"Joey T., look what I'm doing," T.J. called across the room.

Dash frowned. "Not sure you should be calling her Joey T., but maybe Sister Joey T." He waved at the sister, who winked. Obviously, she overheard the conversation.

"I thought you might want some company, Tommy J. Your aunt told me you were reading, so I figured you were here," Sister said. She looked at Dash. "If you have other things to do, I'm happy to stay with your son. We'll come down for lunch and can meet with you then."

Dash nodded. "Thank you. I'm trying to wrap this up. All those tiny details. Did you hear about the man we found in the snowbank?"

When Sister nodded, he asked, "Any chance you popped in and recognized him?"

"No, but you need to ask Edith from the reception desk. Mind like a steel trap, and she does see everyone who comes and goes. Maybe she'll know who he is."

Holding up a finger, Dash said, "Ah, right. Suppose I would have eventually thought of that. Feeling a little sleep deprived right now. Thanks for babysitting." Seeing the look on T.J.'s face, he corrected himself, "Thanks for young-man-sitting."

Dash hurried to the reception area, wondering if anyone would be on duty since the weather made it obvious no one would be traveling out to visit.

Sister Edith was at her post, busy fielding calls from concerned relatives. Her fingers were flying fast and furious punching in the various room numbers. She looked up when Dash stopped at her station.

"Yes, Colonel, or is it General, sorry but I forgot your rank. What can I do for you?"

"Forget the rank and just call me Dash or Hammond, whichever suits your fancy. And what you can do is take a look at a man we found in a snowbank outside the drawing room. Miri Pat says he looks familiar, like someone who attends Mass here on Sunday. Can you spare a minute?"

Sister took off her headset and backed her chair around so she could move from behind the desk. She followed Dash down the hall to the makeshift recovery room. The man lay asleep. She hoisted herself into a standing position, Dash at the ready. Sister leaned over to get a better look.

She wrinkled her face. She nodded toward the door, so they exited.

Billy waited in the hall. "What's the verdict, Sister?

"That's Tater," Sister said.

Billy stared. "As in tater tot?"

Sister sighed and started to drive back to the reception desk. "No, as in Tatum Boone. Tater is his nickname and might be the only name he answers to. Nice enough but not the quickest kid on the block. Pretty sure he has an uncle living in the apartments. Delmar Boone, unless I'm mistaken. Check with Annalise; he might be kin. I've only been here five years and it seems like everyone is somebody's kin. Don't have the family trees in front of me to be certain."

She settled back into her spot and picked up the headset. "Is that enough?"

Both Dash and Billy nodded. "More than enough. Thank you very much," Dash said.

In the hall, Billy said, "Might be kin? Ka-Ching! I do believe all the little pieces just fell into place. Agree?"

Pacing back and forth, Dash replied, "Maybe. Possibly. Probably. Let's find Jumbo and Tiny to see if they gathered any more information. I would have thought that you, the lawyer, would want all the facts before going to court. Innocent until proven guilty."

Billy snickered, "Ah, that's just something they go on and on about in law school. Right now, I just want to punch the guy or gal who made me sick. And I can't believe you don't want to punch someone for messing with T.J. and Mae."

Dash guided his cousin toward the staircase for the walk to the second floor.

"Don't worry, dear cousin. The guilty will not go unpunished, not if I have a say in it. Wonder what Marie has in store for lunch? I'm starving."

"Ah, the army marches on its stomach." Billy said as he laughed.

They reached the stairs when they heard an overhead announcement, "Would Colonel Hammond please come to reception? Colonel Hammond to reception, please."

They did an about-face and walked back to Sister Edith's desk. Standing in the reception area was Ollie, fairly covered with snow. He stood on the mat, clearly not wanting to drip on the marble floor.

Seeing the distressed look on Ollie's face, Dash stepped quickly over to him.

"Ollie, is there a problem? I take it that the snow plowing isn't going well."

"Sir, I found a car, door open. No one inside but it had been running for a while. The exhaust melted the snow all round it. Several empty bottles were inside. I figure the driver got drunk and then left the car. I pulled this out of the glove compartment, but I can't find the driver." He handed Dash a slip of paper. It was the proof of insurance that the state requires each driver to keep in the car. "If that slip is true, then you might have a problem. That guy is a real low-life, trouble with a capital T."

Billy stepped over to read the slip along with Dash. The name of the insured was Tatum Boone, address in Bardstown.

"Well, this confirms the identity of the man in the snowbank," Billy said.

"Man in the snowbank? What's happened here?" Ollie asked.

Dash reached for the man's coat and gloves. "Wipe your feet, and let's talk."

The men adjourned to the restroom down the hall since Ollie did not want to drip all over the wooden floor. Each man picked a spot on the wall to lean against. Dash told an abbreviated version of what happened since they arrived. No mention made of Sister Miriam Patrice's calling in reinforcements for the strange happenings. Ollie was left to assume the problems were the handiwork of this Tater fellow, though the reasons to scare the Hammond group were left unanswered.

Ollie frowned. "I thought I saw a good-sized man around the backside of the building. Figured he was helping the sisters during the storm. Thought he replaced the Borland brothers. They've been out sick for a bit now."

"The man you saw is one of my team, definitely here to help the sisters. You can see why I was so abrasive with you. I figured you might be the guy playing nasty pranks on us. Would you know this Tatum Boone if you saw him?" Dash asked.

"Know him? Yes, sir, I would. I put him in the hospital a year or so ago. Bit slow on the uptake, but has an eye for the ladies. He stalked my Mona, harassed her no end. I had to put a stop to it when he broke into her apartment. Where is he? I'll have a look."

Billy asked, "Did you do jail time for the assault?"

"Nah, the sheriff didn't even charge me. Everyone knows Tater deserved to be beaten a good one. Thought for a minute I was going to get a medal," Ollie said as he started down the hall.

"Small town justice," Billy commented.

They walked to the makeshift hospital ward.

Irma and Ilene were standing guard as requested. Dash whispered the introductions.

Ollie walked over to Tater who was sound asleep. He turned to Dash and nodded. "That's Tater for sure. What happened to him?"

Dash answered, "We suspect he was outside last night during the storm. Since you found his car and the empty bottles, we can assume he spent the night there. Once the gas ran out, he made his way to the building but couldn't get in. Billy spotted him and we dragged him in through a window, which reminds me—I'll have to repair that before it gets dark."

"He had no ID on him, but Sister Edith thought he might be Tater but wasn't sure. You've confirmed it," Billy added.

"If you need to take him to the hospital, if you feel obligated, I guess I can plow a way to the highway. If it were up to me, I wouldn't bother. Good riddance, as they say."

"My wife is a doctor, and she doesn't think he has to be moved right now. The frostbite is being treated; he's resting and after he gets some food in him, he should be okay. I mean, after the frostbite heals. The shelter of the car saved his life. I, for one, want to know what he was doing here so late that he got caught in the storm. Why didn't he phone for help?"

Ollie dusted invisible dirt off his pants. "Guess I should get back to plowing. Snow ain't melting today. I'm trying to make a pass around the building in case anyone wants to take a stroll. Is that your Hummer out front?"

"No, that belongs to the guys helping me. If we have to take Mr. Boone to the hospital, we'd take the Hummer. That shouldn't get stuck." He started for the door and then said, "My car and my wife's are in the carport behind the church. Any chance you can clear that for us? That would help if we can get out of here tomorrow."

Smiling, Ollie said, "I bet Tater has never been called Mr. Boone before. That's his uncle's name. Mr. 'Let's overdevelop the land' Boone. Awful guy. He's been hounding me to sell my piece. He'd like nothing better than to get the sunflower meadow and the land west of that. Has plans, does our Mr. Boone."

Dash and Billy exchanged looks. Could the pieces fall into place any faster?

"Hey Ollie, before you go, is there any lumber in the barn I could use to cover the window I smashed?" Dash asked.

"Better than that, Mr. Hammond. There are three or four replacement windows in storage. Mr. Dowd had the good sense to get extras years ago just in case one cracked. I'll fix it for you before I finish plowing."

"Can't thank you enough," Dash said.

Just a nod, and Ollie was off.

"What's next?" asked Billy.

"Find Tiny and Jumbo. No sense them looking for the car that Ollie already found. And we need to meet this Mr. Delmar Boone and have a word or two with Sister Annalise."

"Annalise has still not appeared over here. I bet she's with her uncle."

CHAPTER TWENTY-FOUR

Dash and Billy met Tiny and Jumbo in the hallway near the exit that Tiny used rather than going through the window.

"Jumbo, I need a few of those bugs you collected and the transmitter. I'm thinking of a bit of tit for tat," Dash said.

Billy smiled. "Since this is so not legal, might I inquire where these little devices are to be placed? If I'm to be party to this activity …"

"Thinking we'll have Irma or Ilene place one or two in Annalise's room. That way we'll know when she returns to her room."

Tiny asked, "This lady talk to herself?"

"Maybe, maybe not but we'd hear the door open and someone moving around," Jumbo answered.

"And William and I will pay a visit to the uncle who lives in the retirement center. A little meet and greet. The counselor here will do the pretty while I plant a bug or two. We will know if Annalise visits him and, hopefully, we can convince Tater to move to his uncle's place. Might be interesting to eavesdrop on Tater's explanation to his uncle about any and all clandestine activities. What say you, team?"

The trio nodded.

"I'll get the bugs. Where do you want to set up the listening station? One of the offices upstairs would work as a central spot. We could tell the sisters we've decided to use it as our bedroom. Bet they'll steer clear after that," Jumbo offered.

"Ilene and Irma are downstairs with the patient. Once I have the bugs, I'll stop in and ask them to deliver them to Annalise's room. Let's hope the door isn't locked. If not, I hope they remember how to pick a lock. A little thing I taught them one boring afternoon," Dash said. "I'll bring Mae up to snuff on this."

Dash's phone pinged. A message from Ilene: Patient awake, sitting up.

Billy looked over to read the message. "I take it we should head that way and have a little talk with Spud?"

"Tater, not Spud, though not sure what difference it would make," Dash said as they headed back to the makeshift hospital room.

The office-cum-infirmary had changed since the men last visited. Ilene and Irma arranged the furniture, so the patient had a corner to himself. The meeting table had towels, medicine and Tater's cleaned and dried clothes. The wet shoes were tucked under a chair, left to dry.

The Tydie Sisters sat at the end furthest from Tater to give him a bit of privacy.

Dash and Billy entered the room, nodded at the sisters and walked over to the far corner.

"How are you feeling?" Dash asked.

The man just shrugged.

Dash turned to Billy, "William, in your own time." He moved back to join the Tydie sisters.

The counselor walked over and squatted down in front of Tater. Closer to eye level, he felt he could better gauge the man's truthfulness.

"Sir, remember me? We met when you first regained consciousness. Does that ring a bell?"

Again, the man shrugged.

"Do you remember your name now? Where you live?"

Tater straightened himself up a bit, but remained seated. "I told you before I don't remember nothing." He became agitated. "You can't hold me against my will. Ain't legal."

Irma smiled, "Can't remember your name, but you remember the law."

Dash stepped forward, towering over Tater. "Oh, I'm sorry. Do you think that's what's happening here? No, sir, no, you are very free to go." He turned to Ilene, asking, "Are those his over there?"

Ilene picked up the stack of clothes and handed them to Dash. "Sorry, but his shoes are still damp. His coat and hat are over there."

The clothes were set on the floor in front of Tater. "You can go whenever you like. If you are hungry, we'll get you some food, then off you go."

Billy stood, ready to follow Dash to the door.

Irma said, "We'll leave as well. Give you some privacy. Are you hungry? Because I'll get a tray for you."

"Hey, wait a minute," Tater shouted. "Where's my car? How am I supposed to get home?"

Billy pulled over a chair and sat down, elbows on his knees, fingers intertwined. He leaned forward. "Oh, you have a car. And a home."

"Of course I have a home; doesn't everyone? And you need a car to get out here. How else would I get out here? Walk? It's over three miles into town."

"You see his car, Dash?" Billy asked.

Dash shook his head. "No, sir, do you know where you left it? I'd be happy to look for it. By the way, I'm Dash Hammond, the man who pulled you out of the snowbank." He extended his hand.

Tater frowned, looking at his red blistered hands. "Sorry, can't shake. Don't even know if I can hold a fork. I'm starving. Do I have to walk to the dining hall, or is that lady going to bring me a tray? A guy doesn't have to freeze to death around here; he just starves."

He stared at his hands. "What am I going to do about these? Can you get me to a doctor?"

Smiling broadly, Dash said, "Oh, I sure can. My wife is a doctor. Let me give her a call. She treated you, which is why your hands haven't fallen off. She's very competent." He pulled out his phone never taking his eyes off Tater. No reaction.

"Ladies, let's see what we can get for Mr. No Name to eat while he's dressing. Billy, if you would please act as his valet, I'm sure he would greatly appreciate it."

Dash, Irma and Ilene left the room.

Left alone with Tater, Billy fussed around with the towels and tubes of cream.

Tater didn't move. "Is that guy the soldier? He seems very military to me. Camouflage pants and all. Dangerous even. He have a gun?"

Billy scoffed, "The soldier, no, no, only a soldier, retired now. He's dangerous only in his own mind. A real pussycat, my cousin Dash." Billy tapped the side of his head. "A bit nuts now and then. Brain injury, but we keep a close eye on him."

He moved the medicine around the table. Not looking directly at Tater, he continued, "The one to watch in that family is his wife. Hell hath no fury like a woman dropped on her head. Unbelievable as it seems, that's what happened to her yesterday. And someone stole her son's favorite toy. Again, stirred up the old maternal feelings. Never knew they could run so deep or be so vindictive. Mean streak. 'Irish witch' is what they call her back home. Oh, don't let that bother you. She is an excellent doctor."

"It's that red hair, isn't it. That's what my mama always said. Red-headed women are the worst, temper-wise." Tater offered, shivering.

"Cold, are you? Need another blanket? Whatever you need," Billy said.

"What I need to do is to get out of here."

"As soon as Doctor Summers says you can move, I'll help you."

The door opened and Irma carried in a tray with a bowl

of hot soup, crackers, and a small dish of cut-up fruit. Ilene carried a bottle of water and a glass of iced tea.

"Would you want to sit at the table? Might make it easier to eat. Can you handle a spoon and fork, or shall I help you?" Ilene asked.

Wrapping a blanket around himself, Tater pushed himself up. A bit unsteady on his feet, he shuffled over to the table and plopped down.

Ilene slid the tray over, opened the water bottle and offered the spoon to Tater.

The injured man folded his hand around the spoon and started to eat. Slurping the broth, he sighed. "This is very good. Or maybe I'm just very hungry."

Billy pulled his chair over. "Probably a bit of both. Chow down, and then we'll finish talking."

Tater squinted at Billy. "Hoping you'd forget about that." He glanced toward the window where the sun bounced off the snow, blinding anyone who stared at it. "Are the roads clear? How much snow is there?"

Irma answered, "Weather reports are saying sixteen inches but there are some drifts as high as three feet. Roads are impassable now, but a warming trend is expected overnight so tomorrow should be much better for travel, if you're up for it." She moved to stand by the door waiting for Tater to finish.

Billy pulled out his phone, reading his messages. "Ah, the good Doctor Summers should be here soon. She'll get you into tip-top shape straightaway."

Tater pushed the tray away. "I'm finished. Look, I really need to get going."

"And where might that be? And how will you get there? Walking is out, even if you were in the best of health. Any other solutions?"

A knock on the door saved Tater from answering.

"May I come in?" Doctor Summers asked. She entered before anyone had a chance to reply. She surveyed the room,

Billy looking a bit sly. Tater looking a bit terrified. Irma and Ilene looking very professional. Feeling like an actor who entered the play without a script, she smiled at each one in turn.

Walking over to the table where Tater sat hunched over his tray, she pulled out a chair. "I'm very happy to see you awake and alert. How are you feeling?"

He glanced warily at her. "Fine, just fine, except for my paws, I mean my hands. They ain't going to fall off, are they? That soldier guy said they might. He as mean as he looks?"

Mae looked over at Billy, who just smiled. "I'm sure you misheard him. You're going to lose some skin, but not your hands. When you're finished eating, you need to visit the bathroom. After all that, I'll clean your hands again, rebandage them. And we'll check your face and ears. Really, sir, not having a hat or scarf or gloves was a very bad thing. Lucky you had shelter, or you'd be dead."

Tater looked down at the tray. "I heard you got hurt yesterday. Sorry to hear that. Bet the guy didn't mean to hurt you." He looked up at her. "Things happen, don't they? Like me losing my hat and gloves, accident. Nobody took them, just lost them."

Not sure how to respond, the doctor just smiled. "Eat up, and we'll tend to your wounds."

She rose and nodded at Billy to follow her out the door.

In the hall, she asked, "What have you and Dash been telling him? His hands are going to fall off? That I was injured yesterday? What should I know before I go back in?"

"Not much. He still claims he can't remember his name, though he remembers having a car and that his home is in town, too far to walk, especially in this weather. He asked if Dash was 'the' soldier so he's party to the bugging. Also knows your dearest is carrying a gun. Knew you had red hair, but seemed surprised you got hurt, so that bit to you is as good as an apology."

"Okay, at least I have some idea now ..." Mae said as

she turned to go back inside.

Billy grabbed her arm. "I guess I should add that I told him you were the dangerous one, Irish witch and all. Very upset about being dropped and then there's the Petey Rabbit thing."

"That all, William?"

"Well, I might have said Dash was a bit nuts, due to a brain injury. Pretty sure that's all."

"Okay, do you want the good doctor or the mad-as-a-hatter doctor when I go back in? Just what are you and my nutty husband trying to achieve? You want a confession? I can get one out of him without inflicting a bit of pain." She shook her head as he opened the door.

With her biggest smile and best bed-side manner in place, she regained her seat next to Tater.

He eyed her cautiously, remembered his ma always smiling before she whacked him upside the head.

Dash hooked up with Jumbo to retrieve some bugging devices. He gave several to Irma with instructions where to plant them.

"ASAP if possible. If Annalise is in her room, do the wellness check bit, plant a bug if you can, and then scram. Billy and I are going to visit this uncle of hers and Tater's. Nice work with the patient. Return to him. See if Mae needs any help. I'll send Tiny down for back-up and a male presence to make Tater more comfortable."

Irma snorted, "Like Tiny's presence is going to make anyone feel better. You're the boss, boss. I'll report back. Where's the listening station going to be, just in case I need some entertainment?"

"Miss Irma, I'm beginning to realize why your superior felt it in their best interests if you left. Second floor, first door. Jumbo will be there."

Irma went off on her errand just as the door to the office opened and Mae exited.

"Dash, can I talk to you for a minute?" she asked.

"Sure," he answered, wondering if this was going to be about T.J. and his whereabouts.

Billy looked at the two of them. "Shall I leave, or should Dash hire me as his defense counsel?"

Mae smiled, "He just might need one." Turning to her husband, she said, "I'd like an explanation about those women who asked you to leave, and you refused. You do know that can be construed as sexual harassment or worse."

Dash sighed in relief. Not about T.J. He smiled at his wife, a laugh about to break forth. "Let me say that 'women' might have been a bit of an exaggeration. Not one to brag ..."

"But you will," interrupted Billy.

"Yes, I will. There was only one woman who ever asked me to leave." He tilted his head staring at his wife. "And that, sweetheart, was you. During what I called our ping-pong period."

"Me! Ping-pong? What are you talking about? I don't remember ever telling you to leave. Hell, it was hard enough to get you home."

Dash raised a finger. "Let me remind you of the divorce you initiated because I couldn't, wouldn't stay home. Military obligations and all."

"Oh, that old bit. Yeah, yeah, thought the military would think you deserted and then you'd wind up in Leavenworth. Had to be better than combat," Mae said.

"Little do you know of prison life," Billy said.

"Anyway, dearest, after you divorced me, you had second thoughts so you wrote, called, cajoled me into coming home whenever I could so I did. Then you'd pick a fight and demand that I leave. Well, I did for the first few times, but you'd always call, cry, etc. and I'd return for a day or two of bliss. The cycle would start over: 'Get out you bastard,' etc. One day I just said no, I wasn't leaving. You could wiggle your little finger all you wanted. The dumb one in all this is me. Should have said 'Too bad, so sad' the first time. Slow learner."

Mae smiled broadly, "Really, I'm the only woman to kick you out? And you came back repeatedly? Guess you really do love me."

Dash stepped over to the wall and banged his head on it. "Billy, make her go away."

Mae walked over to her husband and put her arms around him, kissing his back. "I do love you, Dashiell Hammond. Now I think I will find our son. You didn't lose him again, did you?"

"He's in the Reading Room with Joseph Thomas. They're best buds now." He turned around and kissed her forehead. "Scram, William and I have work to do so we can get the hell out of here."

Mae sashayed down the hall, waving backhanded at them.

Dash looked at his cousin. "Don't suppose I can convince you to trade wives with me?"

"Love Maevis to pieces, always have, but marry her? Knew when we were about five she would be trouble, so I let nature take its course. Twice!" Billy laughed as he started down the hall. "Only one woman said no to you, my Aunt Fanny."

CHAPTER TWENTY-FIVE

Dash and Billy stood outside Delmar Boone's door. They had agreed that Billy would do the talking while Dash wandered around, planting bugs as he went.

They knocked. Nothing. Knocked again.

"Hold your horses, I'm coming," Boone yelled as he pulled the door open. "Who the hell are you?"

"I'm William McCafferty and this is Dash Hammond. We're visiting my sister, Sister Miriam Patrice. Right now, we're looking for Sister Annalise. We're told she's your niece and might be here checking on you. May we come in?" Billy said.

Boone looked from one man to the other and decided he might as well let them in. He swung the door wide and stepped back.

The apartment was very neat, well-appointed as Marie might say. The walls were a cream color, better to set off the pictures and posters that covered most of the large wall. The window overlooked what would be the garden area once the snow had melted and spring had sprung.

"Have a seat, gentlemen. May I ask why you are looking for Annalise, who isn't here now, but did visit earlier? She's very good about checking on me. Worries too much," Boone said.

Billy took a seat while Dash studied the poster, which was the focal point of the wall.

"Can I ask about this—it's a plan, but for where? Looks

like it could be of Marianwood. Oh, that's right. Miri Pat said you were the architect for the conversion of the old dorm rooms into apartments," Dash said, as he turned back to his host.

Boone moved to his side. "Yes, that's what I ultimately envisioned for the land, but was voted down by the congregation. My thought was to construct a little village. Shops, restaurants, condominiums. The motherhouse would sit in the center, a jewel in the crown."

Billy joined them. "I'm on the advisory board now, but don't remember this proposal ever coming forward."

"Oh, it was about ten years ago that I first designed and presented this."

"Did you do the rendering? This is worthy of a frame for sure. Very nice work. Very precise," Dash said.

"I agree but no, I didn't do this. My niece Annalise did it for me. She studied a bit of art and architecture at one point. Kind of a hobby. I was disappointed when she decided to be a mere teacher."

Billy took the cue. "Mr. Boone, tell me more about your plans. The board meets in April, and I do believe finances will come up as always."

Dash asked, "And did you design the individual apartments here? Mind if I look around?"

"Look around. Can I interest either of you in a bit of a mid-morning pick me up? Helps to get the brain cells moving on a freezing day."

Billy declined, but Dash agreed that a finger or two of bourbon was just what the doctor (not his wife, for sure) would recommend.

Boone poured the drinks. He settled into a chair next to the window which he opened just a tad. Pulling out a cigar, he lit it, exhaling the smoke through the crack.

Billy frowned. "Surely smoking isn't allowed. What if you're caught? Would you get kicked out? Can you get kicked out?"

"Nah, to the getting kicked out. Part of my agreement to do the design was a life lease here. And yes, this is verboten but I'm not going to live forever. Need to enjoy the little life I have left. Only one a day, that's all." He took another draw on the cigar. "Now, let's talk about the good sisters and its finances and how I can help them."

Dash sipped his drink and wandered into the kitchen. Then he visited the back bedroom. This was obviously a visitor's room. The furniture was worn and the twin beds had older spreads on them. This was in sharp contrast to Boone's room, where the bed was one of those expensive adjustable beds. A massive television mounted on the wall. This room was a combination man cave and bedroom. A quick glance into the bathroom where he planted the last of the bugs. The apartment was well covered. Every cough and sneeze would register back at the listening station.

The men spent a half hour with Boone. As they were leaving, Dash turned to their host.

"Mr. Boone, a man who could be your nephew, Tater, was found in a snowbank. He doesn't know his name, but a couple of people told us that's who he is. He has frostbite on his ears, face, and hands. In no state to go to his home on his own. Mind if we bring him up here to spend a night or two with you? He'd be more comfortable."

The look of shock on Boone's face could not have been faked.

"Tater. How did he end up in the snowbank? I haven't seen him for a few days. How badly is he hurt?" he asked.

"My wife is a doctor, and she says he'll make a full recovery. He's in a bit of pain right now. Pretty sure she was giving him something for it and hoping he'd get some more sleep. Again, sir, can we bring him to you?"

"Yes, yes. I'll ask Annalise if she can come over and cook. I usually have frozen dinners. Tater hates them. But, by all means, bring him here. Let me give you my number so you can alert me when you'll be here. I'll put away the cigars and booze. Tater likes a sip or two, but can't stop once he starts. In his condition, it's probably not wise to drink."

Both Dash and Billy agreed with that statement. After assuring Boone that they would alert him before they transferred Tater to him, they departed.

A few steps down the hall, Dash touched Billy's arm to stop him.

"Let's give Annalise a few minutes to get out of the closet and we'll surprise her."

"Annalise is in a closet? You sure about that?" Billy asked.

"It's either her or one big mouse. Almost squeaked when I moved around the second bedroom. Thought she might jump out to scare me," Dash answered.

Billy shook his head. "No, let them be. I want to get back to Tater, and you should get back to Tiny and Jumbo. There is still the matter of the noise in the church. We really shouldn't leave without discovering if it is part of the harassment plan, or a forewarning of bad architecture. Hate to have the church fall down around them one Sunday."

"Point well made. Lead on," Dash said, falling in step with his cousin.

Back in the main building, they parted ways. Billy headed to Tater, and Dash, unable to resist checking in on the listening devices, headed upstairs.

He opened the door quietly, since he could hear voices. Unsure if there were people in the room or this was the recording, he peeked around the corner.

Irma broke out into a big smile, waving him over to the station.

"Two seconds after you left, Annalise shows up and can't shut up about all this. She must have been right outside to get inside so quickly."

"She was inside all along, hiding in a closet. Is she still there or can you rewind the tape for me?" Dash asked.

A few seconds of whirring and a click brought the tape to the beginning:

Annalise: Uncle, is Tater okay? I couldn't quite hear everything, but it sounded like he was hurt.

Delmar: That fool got drunk and spent the night outside somewhere, probably in his car. Must have had some shelter or he'd be frozen now. Got frostbite and now those stupid folks are treating him. I can't tell whether they realize who he is, and what he's done or not.

Annalise: Stupid, they are not. I am so sorry I let you talk me into this. I never wanted anyone hurt. Now that doctor got her head banged and poor Tater is frozen. I better get over there if those two are searching for me. They won't stop until they find me. I'll turn up, and then head to my room and ask God for forgiveness.

Delmar: Then do it and stop whining to me. I'm cursed with an ineffective family. You, the holy one, and Tater whose holes are all in his head. Get moving, girl.

Irma leaned back in the chair. "Well, boss, what do you think?"

"Don't call me boss, and you can guess what I think. Time to put pressure on the weak link: Annalise. Your usual excellent job. Will this thing record without someone monitoring it?"

"According to our expert, Jumbo, he set it to start recording when a voice is detected, not just any sound. I'll give you an update if there is one when I see you for lunch. Understand Chef Marie is making her famous lasagna. Makes me hungry just thinking about it."

Dash smiled and nodded. "Yes, yes, indeed. Lasagna. Thank God for Marie. See you downstairs in a bit."

He stopped by the office to see how Billy and Tater were doing. Just fine from what he could see, so he went in search of his wife and son.

Both were in the Reading Room, chatting with Sister Joseph Thomas. He waved at his family and walked over to the church.

Jumbo and Tiny were hard at work searching for speakers, transmitters, or anything else that would broadcast the tap-tap-tap sound. They had a very tall ladder propped against one of the walls. Jumbo was at the top, feeling around one of the light fixtures above one of the Stations of the Cross. Tiny secured the base of the ladder.

Dash walked over to them for a progress report.

"We found a transmitter in the room where the priest gets dressed. So, we have the source, and now we're trying to locate the speakers. Might as well do the job right," Jumbo said.

"Most definitely. Any ideas how many and where?" Dash asked.

Tiny answered, "Sister Bernie, you know, the very old woman among the old women, gave us some clues about where she has heard the noise. The sly old dame moved around the church to locate the sound. Pretty sharp, that one."

Dash nodded and added, "Though I'm not sure I would call her a sly old dame to her face. Then again, she might think it apropos. I'm going up to the choir and then down to the cellar. Don't leave without finding me, just in case."

"Roger that," Jumbo responded.

Dash climbed to the choir loft. A nice organ occupied center stage. He poked around, sticking his hand into every crevice. Nothing found.

He walked over to the railing and surveyed the church. It had just enough architectural elements to set it apart from a plain Protestant chapel. According to Sister Agnes Marie, Harris was a thoroughly distasteful man. He was very strict and built a chapel/church and required his family and the tenant farmers to attend services every Sunday. Attendance was mandatory. Sister had searched but couldn't find any sketches or photos.

The Sisters of the Blessed Mother of God used the smallish church as the foundation for their new church, built with money left to them by Miss Victoria. Nothing ornate, but well-appointed.

Deciding it was time to descend into the cellar, Dash made his way down the stairs to the main floor and then down the next set of stairs.

He wrinkled his nose at the dank smell. He flicked his flashlight on and moved the spotlight around in a very organized manner. Slowly, he walked the perimeter, looking for signs of water damage. He inspected the ceiling in a like manner. Feeling good that he found no signs of impending doom, he turned his attention to the floor.

He moved across it in a grid pattern. The dirt floor was smooth and undisturbed. Why they decided to build a cellar was just another question in the growing list of questions he wanted to ask. As far as he could tell, the space wasn't used for storage, so why have it?

Finally, he felt finished with the task and started to cross the room for the steps. He stopped abruptly. He heard a noise. Not the tap-tap-tap Miri Pat described. This was more like a scratching sound.

Standing still, he reviewed in his mind his survey of the cellar. The scratching continued. He closed his eyes in an effort to concentrate his hearing. After a few minutes, he determined the sound was coming from beneath the floor.

A chill ran down his spine.

Protestant churches often contained graves of parishioners buried beneath the floor.

Dash looked around carefully, wondering if an ancestor of Harris had been buried down here. It took him a minute to realize what he was thinking: that a spirit, a ghost, or whatever term you wanted to use was trying to attract his attention. He held his breath, waiting to hear his name being called.

Nonsense, he told himself. You don't believe in ghosts,

and they surely don't believe in you. It was a rodent, that's all. It's caught down here and is burrowing its way out, or dumber still, was one burrowing its way in. That's the explanation and he was sticking to it.

He hurried over to the steps, vowing never to think of this again. William would have a field day if he saw his cousin rapidly evacuating this space because of a noise. He took the steps two at a time, only slipping once.

Locking the door seemed a safe and sane thing to do. He'd tell Miri Pat not to worry and no need to visit the cellar again. Ever.

CHAPTER TWENTY-SIX

Lasagna time. He hurried to the dining hall. He needed nourishment. Low blood sugar. That's it. New explanation, one he could live with.

He entered the hall to find he was late. He had forgotten the early time for meals. Frowning, he walked past the empty pans of food.

Scanning the room, he spotted Mae and his gang chowing down. They had pushed several tables together to accommodate everyone. It took little time for him to cross the room.

"Where have you been?" asked Mae.

He pulled over another chair and dropped down on it. "Is it all gone? Lie to me if necessary, or I'll shoot myself. I'm starving and lost track of the time." He looked over at Jumbo. "I thought I told you not to leave without me."

Jumbo shrugged. "We called for you, and then checked the door to the basement. It was locked, so we figured you finished and left."

"The door was locked?"

"Yes, sir. Locked up tight. Don't tell me you were downstairs all this time. Sorry, man, you could have been there forever. Sorry," Jumbo said.

"Not as sorry as I would have been had that been true. No, I locked the door after I left, which was just minutes ago. Door must have been really stuck, though it didn't seem that way when I went down. Oh well, still doesn't fill my stomach."

T.J. looked at his plate, which still had a few bites left. He pushed it over to his father. "Daddy, you can have this. I'm full anyway."

Mae threw down her napkin and pushed the plate back to her son. "Dash, check with Marie in the kitchen. I do believe your absence was noted, and she saved some food for you. God forbid you should go hungry."

Dash jumped up and ran to the kitchen where, as Mae said, Marie handed him a tray with a plate loaded with lasagna, salad and bread sticks. Extra sauce sat in a small bowl.

He kissed her cheek. "You are the best woman in the world. Again, you have saved my life. I was about to cry, thinking I missed your lasagna."

Smiling, he returned to the table. Everyone else had finished, but stayed to watch him devour the food.

After cleaning his plate, he sat back, a silly satisfied smile on his face.

Mae's shoulders started shaking as she watched her husband rub his very full belly. "Are you happy? Do you think you need to lick our plates? That would save some dishwashing water."

He made a face at her. "Sorry, but I was starving. I'm discombobulated. God, I wish we were home. I need a good night's sleep." He looked around. "Well, folks, what's on tap?"

"I think we need a skull session to plot our next move or moves," Billy said, as he made eye contact with everyone at the table.

T.J. was the first to reply. "I need to return to the Reading Room to finish my sketches. Is that okay, Mommy?"

"Yes, darling. But you can't go alone. See if Sister Joseph Thomas will go with you. If not, you'll have to wait until either Daddy or me are free. Can you do that?"

The little one nodded.

"Ladies, gentlemen, let's head upstairs," Dash said.

CHAPTER TWENTY-SEVEN

The team assembled in the room where the recording device sat whirring away. Jumbo stopped it and pressed rewind.

"Do you want to listen to this now, or wait?" he asked.

"Let's talk things through and then we can listen. Adjustments are always on the table," Dash said. "William, you have the floor."

"Thanks. I've been giving this some thought. I'm pretty sure we don't want to pull in the police unless Mae wants to press assault charges." He looked for her response.

"No, I'm thinking it would be hard to prove Tater was the gorilla man. And, more importantly, if we call in the law, we're bound to be stuck here for a few more days. I need to get back to my practice sooner rather than later. These video chats aren't cutting it for me or my patients."

Dash raised his hand. "I second that. No police. So, how do we proceed? After we listen to the tapes, we need to approach Annalise to get her side of things. Really, what was she thinking? Tater, I'm thinking we can intimidate into staying away. Delmar Boone, don't know that he can be intimated so do we need to negotiate with him?"

Billy announced his plan. "After I talk to Miri Pat, I'm calling the county attorney asking if he will issue either a restraining order or a no trespass order on Tater. One or the other should keep him off the premises.

"Delmar Boone, I'm thinking of playing him along. Get his plans in writing and telling him I'll get the board to review at the April meeting. My brother Tommy, the accountant, is the financial brains of the board. Once I know exactly what problems the congregation is facing, and what solutions he might have up his sleeve, I'll be better prepared to talk to Delmar."

Irma raised her hand as if she were in class – long remembered response. "I've been listening to Annalise who is praying for forgiveness aloud, probably on her knees. I've heard a lot of 'mea culpa, mea culpa, mea maxima culpa.' What that means for your lay people is that she is guilty, very guilty, and sorry she did what she did. Thinking Miriam Patrice will be able to convince her to get on the bus or get off and find another vocation." She shrugged. "Just my take."

The group turned to get Dash's reaction, but he had his long legs stretched out in front of him. His chin had dropped to his chest. He was fast asleep.

Mae put her finger to her mouth, "Shhhh! Let's give him a few minutes. Leave if you must, but do it quietly."

Tiny and Jumbo nodded and moved silently toward the door. Irma indicated that she would remain at her post. Billy waved good-bye. He headed off to find his sister and have a good heart to heart.

Dash woke with a start. He sat up straight and looked around, trying to orient himself.

Mae and Irma sat across the room with headphones listening to whatever the bugs had picked up. Hearing the scuffle of his chair, they turned and waved.

He stood up, stretched his back, and walked to join them.

"Anything good? Sorry about the nap but I could use a good eight hour stretch on a decent bed. Unless there is another storm tonight, I'm all for leaving in the morning."

"Jumbo called the highway patrol to check on the

roads. Highways are better, almost clear and dry. It will be getting to one of them that's a bit dicey. The patrol thinks one more day and all the main roads will be passable and safe. So, not tomorrow, but the day after we are on our way."

Irma smiled sheepishly. "Dash, would you mind if Ilene and I stuck around for a bit? Two reasons really. One, this is a nice break from our jobs at Biff's. We aren't complaining, but a spell of contemplation would do a lot to revitalize our spirits. Secondly, I'd like to see the aftermath of all this. Not that I'm being pessimistic, but I do worry whether that Tater dude will keep away from the motherhouse if he's allowed on the grounds."

Dash pulled a chair over but leaned on it rather than sit. "I'm fine with you gals staying. I'll square it with Biff. I know a couple of young vets who could use a job as their breaktime from re-entry into the civilian force. I'll make a few calls. And, if you want, stay until that board meeting in April. Tommy Mac will be coming down and I'm sure he'd give you a lift back home. I can't believe Miri Pat would object. Just make sure this isn't a permanent move. Can't live without my Tydie sisters."

Stepping away from the chair, he said, "Now, Doctor Summers, I guess we should see about getting Tater bud out of here and over to his uncle's. Okay to move him?"

Mae walked to his side. "Yes. I'll pack up some gauze and ointment so he can change bandages if he wants. Definitely let his uncle, the architect of this mess, see what his handiwork has done." She looked up at Dash. "Stop me if I decide to kick the you-know-what out of him."

Irma laughed, "I know the word 'shit' if you want to say it."

"Women, you just got to love them. Lead on, Doctor Summers."

CHAPTER TWENTY-EIGHT

Dash and Mae met with Sister Regina who agreed to lend a wheelchair to transport Tater to his uncle. She also filled a goodie box with medical supplies to give to Tater. A discussion followed about whether they should offer Regina's assistance if Tater were to take a turn for the worse.

"I'd be happy to help even though the man is a troublemaker. May I ask what you intend to do to keep him away from us in the future?" Sister asked.

"William the lawyer is working on that as we speak. Miriam Patrice will have the final say in all this. It's possible she will ask the rest of you what you'd like done with him, short of dropping him into the lake with or without a bullet hole in him."

Regina smiled. "Yes, I heard about your method of disposing of bodies. Your son is the talk of the motherhouse. Nice to have a young mind around. Gives us a new perspective on things."

"I could leave him here for a slight fee. In about a week, his new perspective would wear you out. If I could steal some of his energy…"

Mae waved her hand at the two. "Back to moving Tater out of here. Are we ready? If so, let's do it."

"Who's cranky now?" Dash asked.

Mae shot him a look that reminded him to mind his mouth.

They were surprised when Tater complained about the

proposed move to his uncle's apartment.

"But I don't want to go there. I don't mind sleeping on the floor. The food is very good, and you all have been very kind to me," he whined.

Dash towered over him. "Up you go, Mr. Potato Head. Into the chair and off to visit good ole' Uncle Delmar."

When it looked like Tater was going to refuse, Mae stepped forward. "Listen, either get into that chair or I will give your head a whack like you gave mine."

Tater's eyes opened wide. "Who told you it was me? I didn't do it."

"Ah, a line oft said by you. Listen, Tatum Boone, the jig is up. We know all about the bugs, the plan to upset Miri Pat. And, yes, you probably didn't mean to drop my wife on her head. Problem is you did drop her. Here are your choices and think wisely. One, you get into the wheelchair without a fuss. Two, I let Doctor Summers pat you on the head. Three, and this is my favorite, I throw your fat ass back into the snow and let you crawl back to your home or your car or hell."

Tater studied Dash's face and realized he meant every word of number three. The ex-soldier looked tired and impatient. Fierceness oozed out of him.

Even though Tater had the reputation of being slow, dim, or even dumb, he wasn't without the self-preservation gene.

"I'll go to Uncle Del's. And I'm really sorry about the bump on the head, lady. Really didn't mean to drop you. I just lost my grip. Really I did."

Dash reached down and dragged the man up and into the chair. He whispered to him, "You're damned lucky my wife and my cousin are against violence, because right now I want to shoot something or someone and, in my mind, it ought to be you."

Tater groaned and moaned and almost shrieked but didn't utter a word. Shivering, he cowered in the chair.

Sister Regina, the one with the softest heart, covered

him with blankets, tsk-tsking as she tried to make him comfortable.

Dash took hold of the chair's handles and began pushing toward the door. Mae and Regina followed carrying the supplies.

They made the short journey in silence.

Mae rapped on the door. No answer, so she pounded a bit harder.

"Hold your horses. What do you think? That I'm a teenager who can run to the door?" Delmar shouted through the door.

Boone yanked the door open and visibly shrank. His demeanor was less than welcoming.

"Come in. I suppose I can't refuse to take him, can I? His mother would kill me."

"Uncle Del, I'm really sorry about all this. Sorry I messed up," Tater said.

"Where do you want him? He can walk a bit, but he's slower than you. We've brought some supplies. There's some ibuprofen for pain, and I recommend he get into bed and stay there for several days," Doctor Summers said matter-of-factly.

Dash awaited instructions.

Boone looked around his living room, and then waved his hand toward the bedroom. "Take him in there. I can close the door and pretend he's not here."

Sister Regina stepped forward. "Delmar Boone, you know that is no way to treat an injured person, and kin at that. Now, I'll be willing to help him and you, but unless you change that attitude, you're on your own. I know it's not the Christian thing to do, leave Tater to your mercies, but your nephew has caused all kinds of trouble over at the motherhouse. I, for one, never want to see him again."

Dash wheeled the patient into the guest room. He helped Tater into bed, even fluffing up the pillows.

Leaning over him, Dash said, "I almost feel sorry for you. Your uncle is a piece of crap. Listen, my cousin William, aka the lawyer, will talk to you later tonight. Get some rest."

Doctor Summers and Sister Regina joined Dash.

"How many pills can I take? I just wanna sleep. Stay out of Uncle's way."

Dash went into the kitchen and returned with a glass of water while Mae set the packet of pills next to the bed.

"Take two or three now. And then wait until bedtime or after nine to take more. Your hands and face won't need more ointment today unless you wipe what there's off."

Tater looked at Dash. "I have to use the bathroom. Can you help me?"

Dash rubbed his temples. "Why didn't you say this before we got you settled?"

Mae touched her husband's arm. "Let it go. Just help him."

After taking care of business, Tater once again settled into bed. He took the allotted number of pills and wiggled himself down under the covers, closing his eyes. No thanks, no goodbyes.

Dash parked the wheelchair next to the bed and the trio closed the bedroom door.

"Mr. Boone, William and I will be in touch this evening. Make sure Tater is taken care of at least until then," Dash said.

Sister Regina walked over to the slightly opened window. After closing it, she crushed the cigar. She held out her hand. "The rest of the cigars now! If I find you've been smoking, you'll be out in the snowbank with your nephew. There are rules, Mr. Boone, and you either follow them or get out. Capisce?"

Boone nodded, biting his lip.

In the hall, Dash turned to the women. "That went well, don't you think?" And he reached to shake Regina's hand, saying "Extremely well."

CHAPTER TWENTY-NINE

The rest of the afternoon was filled with tying up the loose ends. Dash checked in with Ollie about Tater's car and what to do with it, if anything.

Dash made out a list of security issues he felt needed tending. He talked with Grady about what locks should go where to secure the building. He made a note to gather all the keys that were floating around. A call to Mr. Dowd to inform him of the proposed changes lasted over an hour as they went over details.

Dowd planned to make it to the motherhouse the next day. He and Dash agreed on an intense session. They invited Ollie, as he had worked his way into Dash's heart.

When Dash found Billy, he was on the phone in Miri Pat's office. Dash took a seat and listened in on the end of the conversation.

"What's up, Buttercup?" Dash asked.

"Buttercup? That's lame even for you. And what is up is this: I've talked to the county attorney. The best course is a restraining order against Tatum Boone, forbidding him from entering the motherhouse. A no trespass notice will also be issued.

"Miri Pat and I have had words about exactly what she wants done. Right now, she is talking to some of the sisters to gauge their reactions to all this. Miri Pat is outraged that Tater felt he could roam around the motherhouse at will. And don't ask about Annalise. They are due to meet," he glanced at his watch, "in about twenty minutes. I'm staying away from that, though I'd love to be a fly on the wall. Don't suppose it's ethical to plant a bug so we can listen in?" He gathered his papers. "How'd it go with Delmar and Tater?"

Dash laughed, "Let's say as relatives go, Delmar is not the one you want. He's reluctantly allowing Tater to recover at his place, but I bet the minute the roads clear our potato man will be out on them. Sister Regina has graciously offered to keep an eye and even help take care of Tater. God bless her!"

Billy stood to move around, work out the stiffness from sitting on the phone for so long. "That leaves Delmar. Dollar-bill Delmar. Greed is the root of all this. 'Delmar Village' is what I read on that poster plan in his room. Looks like he wants to build a mini city with himself as the appointed mayor. The poor sisters would take a backseat and end up with some money, but very little land. I now understand why Miri Pat rejected the proposal years ago."

Dash stood, motioning toward the door. "Coffee, tea, or ice cream? You choose. Pretty sure we shouldn't imbibe while working, though I will admit to a taste for some high-powered liquid," he said with a sigh. "Jumbo apparently got an update on the roads. One more day, cuz, and we are heading north."

"Fine with me. After we take a break, how about another skull session? Think you can stay awake for this one? Pitiful sight."

Sister Miriam Patrice sat behind her desk, rubbing her eyes. Her upcoming meeting with Sister Annalise would be uncomfortable for both of them. What went wrong that the younger sister didn't feel able to approach her with the concerns she had? Why the subterfuge? Why the almost childlike pranks?

Before talking with Annalise, Miriam Patrice decided to ask her brother and her cousin if they had any last-minute advice on handling a malcontent.

A tap on the door stopped any more reflection. Looking up, she saw Billy and Dash peeking around the corner.

"Do you want us to come in?" asked her brother.

Miriam Patrice motioned them in. "Yes; this will only take a minute. I'm finding myself muddled about what to say or how to say it to Annalise. I know she has a good heart, but I'm afraid I'm going to jump down her throat for causing or being party to all this."

The men pulled some chairs over to the desk.

"Billy, what do you do when one of your staff undermines you?"

Her brother smiled. "That's easy. I tell them they either get on the team or they are out on the street. I don't have time for all those shenanigans. To be honest, I do very in-depth interviews so rarely do I have what one might call a 'bad hire.' My staff is small, so everyone has to pull their weight or out the door they go."

"Dash, I know from your rank you commanded a goodly number of men. What did you do when someone undermined you?"

The ex-colonel grimaced. "Miri Pat, depending on how egregious the fault, I did have the option of shooting them." He saw the look on her face, so he added, "Just kidding." He shook his head. "Honestly, this Army is all-volunteer, and our screening of recruits is intense. But, and this is worst case scenario, we hold Leavenworth and years of hard labor over their head. That being said, there are all sorts of gray areas there. The mission is drawn up by our superior officers. On occasion, those of us who actually head into combat will voice a concern or two. Discussion on how best to proceed, but always with approval."

He leaned back in the chair. "If I may, ask Annalise for her side. Let her vent, and then ask the sixty-four-thousand-dollar question."

Miri Pat and Billy both leaned in to hear what that was.

"'What would you do if you were in my place?' Push

until you get a complete definitive answer, as detailed as possible. Then you push back, and hard. Give your reasons for doing whatever your way. If she still doesn't agree with you, tell her you are transferring her out of the motherhouse."

"That's it? Why wouldn't I want to keep my enemies close?"

"Because unless I'm wrong, and I am rarely, she would rather be here than anywhere else. That's your carrot. But listen to her. For all you know, she might have a promising idea rattling around in that brain of hers. Pull her away from good old Uncle Del who is my pick for culprit in all this."

Billy laughed, raising his hand. "Swear to God, I thought for sure you would hand Miri your gun and say shoot her."

Dash's shoulders shook. "Figured she was serious, and I'm saving the shooting for Uncle Del. Like I said he's the straw that stirs this particular drink." He stood. "Anything else? If not, get it going. You're in charge so if you feel out of your depth, which you won't, end the meeting."

"Thank you, gentlemen. I'd invite you to stay, but that's seems unfair. Dash, if I send you a text asking for your gun, you'll know the meeting is going badly."

The men stood, rearranged the chairs, and left, wishing her good luck.

Miriam Patrice put in a call to Annalise asking her to come to the office. The dreaded call to the principal's office.

Annalise must have been in the drawing room across the hall, for it wasn't but a minute or two when she knocked on the door and entered.

Pointing to the chair in front of the desk, Miriam Patrice said, "Annalise, please be seated. I suspect this will be an uncomfortable meeting for both of us. Would you please explain yourself? Why the pranks and worse, since Doctor Summers could have been seriously hurt?"

Every inch the head of the congregation, Miriam Patrice waited; hands folded together in the classic pose.

Annalise sat with her head down. It was minutes before she raised her eyes to meet her superior's eyes.

"You need to understand that it was never my intention to physically hurt anyone. No, I guess I shouldn't just limit it to physical. You, I wanted you to think you needed to step down. If I tell the truth, and I guess I should, I'm not sure you know what you're doing leading us."

"Explain."

"Half of our sisters are over seventy, but we are known for our longevity. Right now, we have several in their nineties. Still, we also have a sizable number still teaching and they will continue for several decades. The problem is this: sure, you have secured the motherhouse for the ones living here now, but what about the young sisters? What is going to happen to them when the money runs out?"

"And will it? You know this how?"

"I know you don't care for my uncle Delmar, but he is every bit as smart as those brothers of yours that you brought onto the advisory board. If I have to choose, I'll believe my uncle over your brothers."

"And just what advice would he give us? What should we be doing that we're not? And why?"

At this Annalise began to stutter, "I'm not sure of the details. They're very complicated and he could explain them better than I can, but he's sure we're not making the most of our assets."

"So, you are backing a plan you can't explain. If you had to present it to the congregation, what would you say?"

"Well, I'd have to study it, prepare …"

"So, you embarked on a campaign to make me think I was losing what few marbles God gave me, but didn't fully understand why you were doing this. How long were you prepared to harass me?"

Annalise swallowed hard. "I'm not sure. Really surprised you didn't give up sooner, or at least seek medical or psychiatric help."

"Oh, my poor dear, we McCaffertys are made of sterner stuff. I called in reinforcements because I was tired of messing around. We, well me, have things to decide and these decisions should not be made while lacking sleep."

The younger sister frowned. "I don't think it was fair to call in this brother of yours, and surely not that Army guy. He doesn't play fair, bringing a gun. What would you have done had he shot someone?"

Miri Pat looked at Annalise and answered as she thought her cousin might. "That depends on who he shot and why. Remember, his wife was assaulted ..."

"That wasn't in the plan. Tater overreacted."

"Next time, choose your compatriots more carefully." Miriam Patrice drew in a deep breath and glanced at her watch. "Annalise, I want you to think about all this. You have two choices: you can get back on board with our current plans, or you can leave the congregation and take your sorry relatives with you."

"But ..."

"No buts, Sister. You have a decision to make, and I'd like your answer by nine tonight. If you decide to stay, I promise you I will listen to your suggestions and concerns. I won't promise a reversal in our current plan, but I do promise a fair hearing of your ideas, not Uncle Del's."

Miriam Patrice stood, signaling the end to the meeting.

Annalise followed her lead, but turned before she left. "Is that all you have to say?"

She nodded. "I said what needed to be said. Now I suggest you either return to your room, or perhaps go to the church and listen to what God has to say on this matter."

Annalise seemed smaller when she exited than when she entered.

Alone, Miriam Patrice allowed herself a smile. She plopped back down into her chair, wondering if she should do a fist pump in the air to celebrate. Instead, she opened the bottom drawer to pull out a bottle of Irish whiskey and a

Waterford tumbler. Just a finger, no ice. Sure tasted good.

Dinner that evening was a jovial affair. The Clover Pointe folks knew they had one more day, and then homeward bound. Irma and Ilene announced their plans to spend some more time with their new friends.

"Hey, little guy, how are you? Where have you been?" Dash asked his son across the table.

T.J. didn't stop shoveling the food into his mouth when he answered. "Daddy, I was working on my window sketches. I want to be sure Grandpa can tell how pretty they are. I want to make Miss Victoria happy."

"And how is our resident ghost?" asked Billy.

Shrugging, T.J. just smiled.

"Is Victoria getting any closer to finding her boyfriend's grave?" Mae asked.

Shaking his head, T.J. answered, "No, mommy, she's not really looking for it. That's just what someone said, but not her. She told me she knows a fresh grave and there wasn't one."

Dash leaned in. "She told you this. When?"

"Yesterday, when I was doing my drawing, she visited me. We had a very nice talk."

Mae punched Dash's shoulder. "I told you there's buried treasure out there, and you scoffed. That's what she's searching for. Treasure, not an old beau. She's a smarter woman than I gave her credit for."

T.J. jumped up, a look of anguish on his face. "No, no. I never said that. I promised Miss Victoria I wouldn't say anything. No, take that back. She's going to get mad at me."

The adults at the table shared looks of surprise.

Billy mumbled, "Shades of *The Shining*."

Dash moved to the other side of the table where his son stood. He pulled T.J. away from the table and led him to a quiet corner. Squatting down, he took his son's hands. "T.J., calm down. Miss Victoria knows you didn't tell. She knows

Mommy just guessed about the buried treasure. I'm sorry I've been so busy, but pretty sure we need some father-son time. How about we spend the rest of the night together?"

"Daddy, I need to talk to Miss Victoria. She's my friend. I don't know if she'll talk if you're there. Since you chased her, she's scared of you; that's why she tricked you with the footprints. Thinks you might be like her daddy. Mean. He got rid of her kitten. But I told her you were very nice."

Dash was dumbfounded. A ghost thinks he's mean. Not sure what to say, he looked up and made eye contact with Mae. A message sent: come. He smiled when she stood and moved in their direction.

"What's up, Thomas? How can I help?" she asked.

T.J. explained again about his promise not to talk about the missing jewelry. "Mommy, she just wants a pearl necklace that belonged to her mommy. Her daddy took it from her."

Dash told Mae about T.J. wanting to visit with Victoria, and that he wasn't welcome since he chased her in the cemetery.

Mae pulled a chair over and then hoisted T.J. onto her lap, cradling the little boy. "Thomas, let Daddy and me talk this over. How about you visit with Uncle Billy for a bit?"

His lower lip moved out and a frown appeared on his forehead, but T.J. nodded. "Okay." He slid off her lap and started to walk away. Turning, he added, "I'm not happy."

Dash was opening his mouth when he caught Mae's look. He pulled over another chair and took a seat.

"Not good to feed this idea of Victoria. Maybe I am mean like her father, but I don't think letting T.J. go on about this is going to help him."

He could see his wife weighing the options.

"Dashiell, what if both of us stay with him? If Victoria doesn't like you, she'll stay away. Thomas will be disappointed, but he will have had a chance. I know you don't believe, or at least say you don't, but deep down in that cold,

cold heart of yours, you understand that maybe, just maybe, spirits do visit with us. Chances are, this whole meeting Victoria was a dream he had. Remember I found him asleep in there this morning."

"This morning seems like a decade ago. Okay, he can accept both of us or no one goes into the room."

With that, they got up to find their son, who was pleading his case to his honorary uncle, the lawyer.

As Dash and Mae approached, Billy and T.J shook hands.

"Good evening, parents. Your son has retained me as counsel. I believe there is some negotiating to be done."

Dash stared at his cousin, trying to convene a message of 'butt out.' Instead, he looked at T.J. and asked, "Do you think I'm mean?"

"No, daddy, but you can be scary. You're very big and when you yell, you are very loud."

This shocked Dash as he always thought of himself as a very amiable, reasonable man. He asked his son, "Are you afraid of me?"

T.J. looked at his mother and then back to his father. Putting his forefinger and thumb almost together, he said, "A little."

Dash's whole demeanor collapsed. "Well, that's made my day, probably the year." He turned and walked slowly out of the room.

"What did I say? Is Daddy mad at me?" T.J. asked.

"Listen, kid, when you pay me to be your mouthpiece, that means you keep your mouth shut." Billy sighed. "No, he's not mad, more like very sad. I think you may have hurt his feelings." He turned to Mae and asked, "Which one of us should go?"

T.J. made the decision for them when he ran after his father.

Catching up with Dash, T.J. grabbed his father, tucking

his little hand into his father's big hand. They walked into the drawing room where they sat down, still holding hands.

"Am I really scary? I know I'm tall, but I'm not big like Mr. Tiny. And I don't yell very often, do I?"

T.J. shook his head. "No, but 'member when you almost broke your hand off smashing that cabinet? You did a lot of yelling that night. Scared Pansy Pup. And me."

"And your grandfather and Uncle Tom and Miss Annie and Grady and a few others. Yes, unfortunately I remember that night all too well. I'm so sorry about ..."

"It's okay, Daddy. Mommy explained that sometimes the terrible things that happened when you were a soldier upset you and you have to yell to get it all out."

"Wise woman, your mother. I do try. How about this? Instead of going to the Reading Room now, we play some games, you and me? Then tonight, if you still want to visit Miss Victoria, we'll sleep in the room. You know she's most likely to come out at night."

T.J. thought it over. "Okay, we don't have a place to sleep anyway, do we?"

"No, the guest house is out and, unless we want to share a room with Jumbo and Tiny who probably snore really loud, the Reading Room is our best bet. Mommy can join us. Now, how much did you pay Uncle Billy?"

"A nickel. Found it in my backpack."

Dash looked up to see Mae and Billy standing at the room's edge watching and listening. "Get your money back. A nickel is a nickel, after all."

The Hammond family settled back in the dining room to play card games all evening. Off and on they were joined by different sisters, who wanted to sit in so they could watch the little guy's winning expression. Soon adults as well as the child were jumping up and down yelling 'slap jack.'

Dash checked his watch, thinking it had to be close to T.J.'s bedtime. This soldier, for one, was exhausted and just wanted to hit the mattress no matter how thin it might be. Tiny had moved several into the Reading Room along with an ample supply of blankets and pillows. Billy insisted on joining them, reminding everyone he was the child's godfather as well as his attorney.

Mae and the little one settled down to Facetime with Grandpa, who had volunteered to read a bedtime story.

Dash checked on his family to find that both wife and son had borrowed tee shirts from his duffel bags to wear as pajamas. Chiding them for taking all his clean clothes, he was left with packing the dirty clothes to be carried home and laundered there.

Tiny and Jumbo volunteered to continue doing rounds even though everyone was sure the gorilla man was Tater, now out of commission with frostbite.

Returning to the Reading Room, Dash found his son sound asleep curled in a pile of blankets.

Mae whispered to him, "He was out before Grandpa finished the second page. Our baby is exhausted. We can't get home soon enough."

"Curl up next to me, and let's get as much sleep as we can." He turned to his cousin. "Say goodnight, Billy. Sleep tight."

CHAPTER THIRTY

Dash woke up. He listened to see if he could determine what sound ended his sleep. His trip to the cellar made him a little more suspicious than usual. He glanced over Mae to see the empty space where their son should be sleeping.

He sat up quietly and scanned the room. T.J. stood before one of the windows, whimpering. The little boy had his hand on the puppy in the window. He joined his son, softly touching his shoulder. He whispered, "T.J., what's the problem? Why the tears?"

"Daddy, I miss Pansy Pup. I want to go home and see Grandpa. My tummy hurts. My head hurts. I want to go home. Can we?"

"Come here, buddy. Let's have a cuddle in the rocking chair, and then crawl back into bed."

As Dash rocked his son, he glanced around the room. In the far corner, he saw a flickering light that gradually grew into a shadowy figure, a lady wearing a long flowing dress and large hat. Miss Victoria wasn't that frightened of him.

He sat, watching the ghost watch him. Finally deciding he was too tired to keep playing games, he stood up, cradling T.J. He cautiously laid him down next to Mae. Lowering himself, he whispered, "Mae, our little boy isn't feeling very good. I think he's a little warm as well. Do your doctor stuff."

Mae moved around to grab her medical bag. She pulled out an electronic thermometer and pointed it at T.J.'s forehead. A slight temperature. She maneuvered her son between Dash and herself.

"Let's get some sleep and see how he is in the morning. I don't want to wake him up. He's just overtired and overanxious. All that ghost stuff."

Dash concurred with his wife by nodding. He didn't want to admit to seeing Miss Victoria. His son wasn't the only one overtired.

The next morning, T.J. was still warm and still had a tummy ache.

Dash tracked down Miri Pat to see if they could use her room so Mae and T.J. could get some decent rest in solitude.

He tucked wife and child into bed, telling Mae, "I'm off to meet with Dowd, the property manager. We're doing a conference call with Grady to review security plans. I'll fill you in when I know what we're doing."

"Just make sure you're not the one hammering and all that. Home tomorrow, with or without you," When Dash didn't respond, she added, "A salute would be good at this moment, Colonel."

"How about a kiss and a promise I'll be the one driving tomorrow?"

"Fair enough. Now get this settled. You've piddled around enough. Men!"

Dash had learned many life lessons over his fifty-some years. The biggest was when to argue with Mae and when to just shut up. He smiled and backed out of the room as his son and wife snuggled down under the covers.

He went in search of his cousin. "William, my man, what's going on?"

"Just got off the phone with the county attorney. I'm taking the Hummer into town to do a face-to-face. Miri should come, since she's the one asking for the restraining order and no trespass on Tater, aka Tatum Boone. I wanted to stop him from coming on the grounds at all, but Miri wants him to be able to attend church and visit his uncle. He just won't be allowed inside the motherhouse."

Dash nodded his head in agreement. "Suppose that's the best you can do. Your sister is too soft-hearted for her own good. She does understand she can't allow him even one misstep?"

The cousins walked down the hall together, separating at the reception area. Billy gathered his coat and gloves while Dash continued on to the office where Dowd and Grady's men were waiting for him. A diagram of the buildings lay on the table, with the doors highlighted in red. The men gathered around to review the plan Dash thought would best secure the sisters.

When Grady joined via Zoom, the details were nailed down. Half the doors would be turned into fire exits with no access from outside, equipped with an alarmed crash bar which would notify the whole building if someone exited. The remaining doors would have keypads. Everyone would get their own code. This would help in tracking everyone as they came and went. Grady also suggested cameras for each entrance, just in case someone's code was compromised.

"Dowd, we'll need an office to set up the surveillance cameras. If twenty-four-hour staffing is possible, then do that. At the very least, someone monitoring it all night," Dash said.

The property manager, not that many years older than Dash, leaned back in his chair, chewing on a toothpick. "Not sure the budget holds for that kind of expense. I mean, all these changes have to cost a good penny. Don't know what to tell you."

"Hang the expense. These changes aren't costing anyone but Grady and me anything. I'm picking up the hardware expenses, and Grady is paying for the labor."

Grady piped in, "Mr. Dowd, Jumbo, and Tiny here will be staying on and helping with security until I can get a few more men and the equipment down there for installation. All you need to do is get heat into that guest house, so my men can stay there rather than in the motherhouse. This will give them more freedom to move about the grounds."

Dowd nodded. "Sure Sister Miriam Patrice is on board with all this? I mean, I have no problem with it other than getting all the dearies to remember their passcodes. Do you want the surveillance room here in the motherhouse, or out in my office? I can find space in either area. What about the Borland brothers? Are they out of the picture? Think they'd want to monitor this from their hut?"

"Good questions, D-man. Your answer," Grady said.

"Right now, the Borlands aren't high on my priority list." Dash held up his hand to stop Dowd from saying anything. "Yes, I know the one can't help getting sick, but the other could have helped by not taking a vacation. I'm thinking this job must not mean much to them." Again, he raised his hand. "Listen, I will defer to you and Miri Pat and the accountant, in that order."

Dowd thought about all this and then asked, "What about Father Greg, as he's called? He'll need a passcode. He always comes in the door behind the altar; he parks right behind the church. Don't think we should change that door into a fire exit."

Dash stood up and walked around the table, clearly upset. He turned to Dowd. "Now, please understand this. I've asked a million times who has keys, and not once has this Father Greg come up." Scratching his head, he added, "I am frankly amazed that there is any gold or silver left in the church, or anything left anywhere in this building. The antiques alone would pay for several improvements, but I do understand the reluctance of the sisters to part with them."

He leaned over the table into Dowd's face. "Sir, would you please draw up a list of everyone not wearing a habit that should have a code? If it turns out to be half of Bardstown or the environs, we might have to produce a different system to track folks."

Grady started laughing. "It is hard to deal with civilians, isn't it, D-man? Hey, let's cross that bridge, however wide it turns out to be, when we see the list. Right now, back to the doors, and would someone tell me why there are so many to start with?"

Dash turned to Dowd. "Mr. Dowd, I apologize. I'm not yet used to lack of control of any situation. Grady, you start on gathering the equipment and send the bill to Tommy Mac. Please don't let Mae see it. My savings account is running on empty right now. Talk to you again soon, G-man. Any final instructions for Jumbo and Tiny?"

"Yes, try not to eat the good sisters out of house and home. Stay in touch."

With that, Grady signed off.

"Mr. Dowd, let's move this to the dining hall where we can get some coffee or something to help us sharpen our minds. Jumbo, Tiny, want to join us?"

"Before we leave, may I say one or two things?" Dowd asked.

After receiving nods from the other men, he said, "I am not as incompetent as you all might think. It's just that dealing with Miriam Patrice isn't easy. Strong-minded, but terribly soft-hearted. She clutches at pennies while dollars might drift away. Several long meetings will sort all this out. Since you've told me a bit of what went on, I have a better picture of the last few months." Under his breath, he added, "If I ever get my hands on that idiot Tater Boone ..."

Dash concurred, then changed the subject. "The guest house. We need to check on it to make sure the pipes haven't burst and, no complaint intended, but why isn't there a generator for that house, since this building is so covered?"

"Not many visitors stay there, especially in the winter. But, and I was getting to this, I ordered a generator yesterday. Should be delivered later today, and I'll get it hooked up. That should provide enough heat, light, and hot water for your men and those coming." Dowd gathered the papers in front of him. "I suggest we head for coffee, and get moving. We have a lot to do."

"Spoken like a real commander, sir. Well said," Jumbo said.

The meeting moved on to the dining hall and more caffeine.

The afternoon flew by as Dash and his team cemented the details of the security system. Miriam Patrice would be presented with a complete and airtight plan. Accompanying the report would be an unquestionable report outlining cost, if any, to the order, and a timeline for installation and training for the sisters and employees so, once implemented, the problems would be minimal.

Mr. Dowd, true to his word, led the men to the guest house since the generator arrived. Together, they hooked it up and began to heat the house. Dash played housekeeper, stripping the beds and gathering towels, replacing them with fresh clean linens he had the foresight to bring from the motherhouse.

CHAPTER THIRTY-ONE

Dash glanced at his phone. A message from Mae: Urgent! Come to the motherhouse, main staircase.

He tucked in the last bit of blanket on the bed. So much for his housekeeping skills. Yelling to Dowd, he said, "I have to get back. Some damned emergency. Would you make sure Tiny and Jumbo do one more sweep for listening devices? Then they can move in. Thanks."

As he walked across the yard, a thousand thoughts ran through his mind. T.J. hurt, though wouldn't Mae have said that? Mae hurt, no. That left Billy. Oh Lord, what happened to him?

He took the steps two at a time and pulled at the front door, expecting it to open. When his hand met resistance, he started to curse. He turned to head back down, but stopped when he heard his name.

"Wait, Dash, wait. I'll open the door," Mae said, unlocking the old door. She pulled it open and grabbed her husband. "Quick, get inside."

Dash surveyed the surrounding area looking for bodies, either dead or maimed.

"Maevis, where's T.J.?" he asked.

His wife pointed to a spot under the elaborate staircase.

He watched as his son peeked around the corner shyly.

Mae shoved Dash toward his son, jabbering, "Listen, it was an accident, but you have to fix it. Embarrassing, to say the least."

Dash stopped to shake his head, hoping that would loosen whatever was impairing his understanding.

Once they were all crammed into a tiny space under the staircase, T.J. brought his hand from behind his back. In it was the newel cap from the mansion's staircase.

"This is the emergency?" Dash asked his wife. "What happened, and just what am I supposed to do?"

"Daddy," T.J. said with a huge sigh. "I didn't do this. Mommy did. She was the one who wanted to slide down that railing. Told her she shouldn't, and that you'd be upset."

Dash's face broke out into a very broad smile. He bit his lips to keep from laughing. He looked at his wife, who he could see was now regretting her call for help.

"You slid down the banister and broke off the newel cap. What possessed you to even imagine, at your age, that a ride down the banister was a thing to do?"

"Don't give me 'at your age.' You do silly things all the time and I don't get on your case."

T.J. tugged at his father's pant leg. "Daddy, this isn't fixing this. When Miri Pat finds out…"

Dash held up his hand. "Stop right there. When Miri Pat finds out, she will burst with laughter. This will go down in the annals of the congregation." Unable to contain himself any longer, he bent over in laughter.

"Stop it this instance, Dashiell Hammond. It's not funny, not one bit," Mae said.

Dash pushed her aside so he could leave the hiding spot. "Oh God, Maevis, it is so funny. Wish I had been here to film it. Why am I never around for these precious moments?"

"Precious moments, my Aunt Fanny," Mae snorted.

"And how is your fanny, my love? Look me in the eye. I just know you have a concussion or whatever one calls it when common sense is knocked out of you."

He moved the family into one of the small parlors at the front of the house. Around the walls small display cases held memorabilia, lined up like little soldiers, from Victoria

Harris.

"Please sit down and start at the beginning. Why aren't the two of you sound asleep in Miri Pat's room?" he asked.

Mae took a deep breath. "Well, we did take a nap, and woke up feeling fine. After a quick stop in the dining hall for a refueling moment, we decided to take this, our last day, to explore the old mansion. Since I read that brochure you got from Sister Agnes Marie, we thought it might be fun to investigate." She stood up to pull the brochure from her back pocket.

"Walk with us," she said as she started for the first box. Opening the pamphlet, she read, "The Harris mansion was begun in 1868 and finished in 1873." She turned and waved her hand around. "These are the original walls, floor, windows and the two settees on the other side of the room are originals as well. That's why you're not supposed to sit on them, like we just did."

"Cut to the chase, Doc. We have work to do more important than this history lesson," Dash said.

Hands on her hips, Mae said, "Sure! When you want to drone on and on, that's important. When Thomas and I want to broaden your horizons, you scoff at us."

"Your lower horizon was broadened by that trip down the railing. Your head hurts, and now your butt hurts. Yin and Yang," Dash said with a smile and a wink to his son. T.J. shook his head.

"Don't 'yin and yang' me or you will never see the yin again. Sex will be a distant memory if you keep yammering on, so zip it, Buster," Mae said.

Thomas pulled on his daddy's hand. "What's sex, Daddy?"

"Something I will never have again if your mother has her way. But never fear, I can talk her round," Dash said, avoiding an answer to T.J.'s question.

Mae straightened herself up. "Gentlemen, shall we continue? Over here we have Victoria's hand-painted cards, which were the patterns for the stained glassed windows in the Reading Room. Take a good look at her handwriting." She waved them on to the last display. "Here is the will that leaves everything, lock, stock, and barrel, to 'my loving daughter, Victoria.' Again, note the handwriting. Very similar to the explanations for the windows."

"You are concluding that Victoria forged a will to get the plantation. Makes sense, though how she switched it with the original begs discovery. That theory does answer the question of how a female inherited such a prime piece of property, lock, stock, and barrel."

T.J. again pulled at his daddy. "Are you going to fix this or not?" A look of despair followed the question. "Sister Miri Pat is going to be mad at me, I just know it."

Dash squatted down to be at eye-level with his son. "Miri Pat isn't going to be angry with you. You didn't slide down the banister. All will be well." He stood to face his wife. "Continue, Maevis."

"Well, remember Thomas saying that Victoria told him she was looking for jewels, not a departed, in every sense of the word, lover? I began to wonder …"

"Was this with the yin or the yang, my dearest heart?"

His wife walked over to one of the settees and plopped down. Her head lowered, but Dash could see a big tear slowly making its way down her cheek. Dammit, he thought, she always pulls out the tear card and he always caves.

He sat down beside her, taking her hand. "I'm sorry. I'm being very insensitive. I shouldn't mock you and your ideas." He wiped away the tear. "Listen, I'll tell Miri Pat it was me who broke the newel cap off. If I can find wood glue, I'll have it fixed in a jiffy."

They both looked up as Sister Agnes Marie rounded the corner from the infirmary wing. She walked over to them, a frown on her face. "Excuse me, but you're not allowed to sit there. Don't tell me you can't read. You're lucky it didn't collapse."

Dash looked up at her and then stood, pulling Mae up as well. "A thousand pardons, Sister. We three Hammonds are having a bit of a problem."

"Such as?" Sister asked.

Dash moved to step forward to explain, but Mae pushed him back, sending him onto the settee. As if to fulfill Sister Agnes Marie's prophecy, the delicate piece of furniture gave way. Dash sprawled on top, his arms flailing about.

He watched as T.J. pulled Sister Agnes Marie's habit. The child said, "Sister, I didn't have anything to do with that or this." And he handed Sister the newel cap.

"Next thing you know, he'll deny knowing us, claiming we kidnapped him from his real parents who are delightfully rule-abiding." As he finished, he caught sight of Billy striding toward them. Rush hour in the motherhouse.

Billy stopped short, frowned, and then said, "Oh there you are. What are you doing? Can't you read?" He pointed at the sign, "You're not supposed to sit on the furniture. Really, Dash. I expected better of you."

Dash watched his turncoat son walk over to his godfather and slip his tiny hand into William's.

"Help me up, and I will explain all. Or at least I'll try."

Billy extended his hand to pull his cousin upright.

Dash looked at the staircase and said, "Let's sit on the stairs. Pretty sure those are safe from a lummox like me. Come along, Sister, you may as well hear this," Dash said as he led the way. Once everyone sat down, he nodded toward Mae. "Dearest, would you like to start, or shall I?"

Mae stood and slowly told the tale of searching for the lost jewels.

Billy raised his hand. "Excuse me, how does sliding down a banister help you find the jewels? Not sure I see the connection." He leaned toward his cousin, "Dash, does this make sense to you?"

Dash, figuring he was in enough trouble with his wife, just shrugged.

"Well, sir, I can see the connection. If we're not looking for a body, but jewels, then the house would be an ideal place to hide them. Right, Doctor Summers?" asked Sister Agnes Marie.

"Right, Sister. Thomas and I were about to start searching when I lost my mind for a moment and decided to slide down the banister." She sighed deeply. "Never thought I'd break something. My apologies, Sister."

Dash sprawled back on the stairs, smiling. His wife in a contrite mode was interesting to watch. He turned to his cousin, whose mental wheels he could almost see turning.

Billy spoke up. "So, we are taking Thomas' word about talking with the ghost and we are believing her story of lost jewels. Mind you, even if we find the jewels, the value would hardly be enough to 'save' them so don't expect that result."

Okay, Dash thought, it was time for him to take charge, add a dose of logic to all this.

Standing up, he turned to the assembly of four. "Listen up, dearest ones, so we are looking for jewels, indeterminate in number and kind. What makes you think Mr. Harris didn't just bury them with his wife? That would partially explain the ghost in the cemetery. Is Mrs. Harris in the mausoleum?" He looked at Sister Agnes Marie for an answer.

"No, she is not. And neither is Victoria. Originally Mrs. Harris was interred there, but when her father died, Victoria removed her mother and buried her right outside the mausoleum. She didn't want her parents to be together for all eternity. But why she didn't bury her father and leave her mother in the mausoleum is another mystery."

"Again, why should we assume the jewels are in the house and in this particular area of the house?" Dash asked.

Mae pulled out the brochure and waved it at him. "If you read this like you say you did, you should recall that this area of the house was completed shortly after Mrs. Harris died, making it a perfect place to hide something valuable that you might want to retrieve quickly. Remember, just because

Harris didn't want his daughter to have the jewels doesn't mean he didn't want them. What if he decided to remarry? A nice gift of jewels to the new wife would sweeten the pie for her, don't you think?"

Dash and Billy exchanged glances. Both knew about their women and their jewels. A 'Get out of jail' card for sure.

"So, gentlemen, ye of the razor-sharp minds, where would you hide jewels?" Mae asked.

T.J. stepped forward holding the newel cap in his hands. "I'd hide them in here, but I'd make this cap a screwed-on thing so I could get to the treasure quickly."

Sister Agnes Marie pointed around the room. "Please take note. The oil-burning lamps were refitted for electricity years ago, so no jewels hidden there. And the chandelier is lowered and cleaned at least once every few years. Again, no jewels."

It was Billy's turn to prowl around the room. He pointed to the collapsed settee. "Don't suppose the furniture was re-upholstered?"

Sister Agnes Marie nodded. "When we did the refurbishing of the room, a decade or two ago, an examination of each piece was done. Then repairs or modernization were performed, if needed. At the time, we weren't thinking of preserving the historical aspects. No plans to open the motherhouse for tours." She shook her head. "I'm sorry to say we weren't the caretakers we should have been. The bedroom that was Miss Victoria's had been divided into two rooms so more sisters would have their own space. I have no idea where Harris hid the jewels."

Dash spoke up, "Back to Mae's point, if Mr. Harris wanted to have the jewels close by and easily retrieved in case of necessity, where would he put them? Suggestions?"

They began to prowl around the room.

T.J. said, "Daddy, check to see if the cap over there screws on. Maybe the jewels are there."

Dutifully Dash checked. He stood to shake his head.

"No, T.J., not here."

It was Billy's turn. He walked over to the post upon which the newel cap would sit. "I'd build a secret door into this so when I needed to get the jewels, I'd just tap it in the right spot and presto, the jewels are revealed." To demonstrate his point, he forcefully tapped the base of this post.

To everyone's amazement, there was a loud click and a small compartment door swung open.

"Incredible. Luck of the Irish, for sure." Dash joined Billy, who knelt down next the compartment. "Go ahead. You found it. Reach inside to see what it holds."

Sister Agnes Marie, Mae and T.J. gathered round the two men.

"Here goes nothing," Billy said as he reached inside. He slowly pulled out a velvet sack. He looked from one of his comrades to the other. Handing the bag to Sister Agnes Marie, he said, "Sister, you do the honors since whatever is in it will belong to you and yours."

She moved to the steps to sit down, patting the next space. "Thomas, come here and help me open this."

The youngster happily complied after tossing the newel cap to his father.

Dash leaned into Billy. "This is too easy. Why didn't the door open whenever the railings and such were cleaned?"

Billy just shrugged.

Sister bounced the bag in her hand. "It's not too heavy, so maybe there really aren't many jewels."

"As long as the pearl necklace is inside, Sister, that's what Victoria really wants," T.J. said.

Sister Agnes Marie turned the bag upside down and watched as a pearl necklace slid out. Following it was a diamond necklace, earrings, and a beautiful emerald ring.

T.J. helped cradle the jewels. He looked to his father. "Daddy, Miss Victoria will be so pleased with us. Can I run to her room and tell her?"

"Any self-respecting ghost should be here invisibly watching us. So stay here. Frankly, I'm tired of searching for people and things." He sat down to reach for the jewels. "Maevis, bring your womanly instincts over here and give us a fair market price for these."

She scoffed at her husband. "Didn't bring my jeweler's loupe, but hand them over."

After examining the jewelry, she said, "Low ball is a hundred grand; top line would be a quarter of a mil. Really depends on the quality of the stones. I can only hazard a guess. This is where you call in a professional." She handed the jewelry back to her husband. "If nothing else, these should be secured until evaluated."

Dash and Billy both looked at Sister Agnes Marie.

"Do you have a secret pocket where you can stash these until Miri Pat can figure out what to do? Since half the sisters have the combination to the safe, I'm not sure that's the place to hide them until what needs doing gets done," Dash said.

Sister took the booty and returned them to the velvet sack. She walked back to the post and tucked the jewels away, shutting the small door with a firm click. "They've been safe there all these years; a few more days won't matter." She dusted off her hands. "Gentlemen, I think we need a sit-down to discuss what's next."

Dash turned to his son. "T.J., this is one of those secrets we have to keep for a bit, and then you can tell everyone how you found the jewels for Miss Victoria. Can you do that for us, for Miss Victoria?"

T.J. nodded. "Can we get some ice cream? That would help me keep my trap shut for sure."

While T.J. devoured his ice cream cone, the four adults sat, heads in hands.

CHAPTER THIRTY-TWO

Phones pinged. Miri Pat wanted to meet with Dash and Billy before meeting the Boones. The men headed in her direction.

Dash opened the office door and there sat Miri Pat behind her desk, looking every inch the leader of the pack, his very irreverent take on the structure of the congregation.

She gestured for them to sit. "I've set the meeting with Tater and Delmar for six o'clock sharp. Dinner is over by then. I'm hoping that keeps everyone calm," Miri Pat explained.

Dash watched as Billy pulled a file from his briefcase, saying, "We have both the restraining and no trespass orders. Still haven't decided what to do about Delmar and his plans for the property, or how I can convince him to follow the proper channels and not harass my sister into anything."

"I'll set my gun on the desk, and Miri Pat can motion to it as her answer to any unwanted persuasive measures. Hey, do you want Mae here? She has a great menacing demeanor. Always scares me," Dash said. He looked to Miri Pat. "You already have your best principal-hand-smacking look on. That should scare any right-thinking person. I still have nightmares about, what was her name, Sister Florence something, not Nightingale. I'm surprised I can still use my hands after all the beatings I took."

Billy burst out laughing. "You poor sod. Not one blow was undeserved. And my personal view is you had the hots for her, and just wanted to be in her presence."

Miri Pat threw her hands out wide. "Stop, you two. Don't go down that lane, dear brother, and as for you, my dear cousin, you were always a menace when you didn't have your nose in a book or were chasing a ball or Mae. If the two of you can't be serious, both of you will be banned from the room during the meeting." She drew in a deep breath. "And please, Dash, no guns, okay?"

The two men nodded.

Dash glanced at his watch. "Time to eat, so let's do it. Been a long day. Over dinner, I'll give you the highlights of the new security system, which needs to be installed as soon as possible. Dowd can give you the minutiae later. And we have news for you; a pleasant surprise, we hope."

Six o'clock arrived. Delmar and Tatum arrived at Miriam Patrice's office. She had taken Dash's advice to hold the meeting on her turf, her comfort zone. Always make the other guy uncomfortable.

Tatum looked like the poster boy for uncomfortable. His frostbitten face, still red and burned, mirrored his hands still bandaged. He huddled under blankets in the wheelchair, hunkered down as if that would help him look pathetic. Him just showing up accomplished that.

Delmar, on the other hand, wore his best suit and pushed the wheelchair into the office with an air of authority, as if he were the one who demanded a meeting.

Dash and Billy sat off to one side.

Sister Miriam Patrice pointed to a recording device on her desk. "Mr. Boone, I will be taping this meeting. Even though it is informal, I feel the need to have a record.

"Sure, sure, you do what you want. I have nothing to hide," said the elder Boone. He pointed to his nephew, adding, "And neither does Tatum."

After parking the wheelchair, Delmar stood facing Sister Miriam Patrice. He nodded toward Dash and Billy. "See you brought in the big guns. Rambo still carrying?" He opened his suit to show a gun tucked into his belt. "Figure we should be on even ground here, gun-wise."

Before Dash or Billy could respond, Sister Miriam Patrice stood up and slammed her hand on the desktop.

"Delmar Boone, what the hell do you think this is? The O.K. Corral? Put that gun on my desk this instant and sit down and shut up."

"I only thought …" as he laid the gun on the desk.

"For the good Lord's sake, Delmar, you didn't think." She reached for the revolver, opened the cylinder and spun it, checking for bullets. Turning it upside down, one bullet dropped out and bounced off the desk. "Pick it up, Delmar," she said with her hand outstretched.

"Where the hell are my bullets?" he asked as he picked up the lone one and handed it to her.

Pocketing the bullet, she sat down. "Sit!" she directed Delmar, who immediately sat. She slid the gun into a drawer in her desk and locked it.

Slouching in his chair, Delmar pointed at Dash. "Bet he gets to keep his gun."

Dash stood, holding his hand out and slowly turned around to demonstrate that he had nothing to hide. He sat down again without saying a word. Then he reached into one of his voluminous pockets and pulled out five bullets, putting them on the desk.

Delmar started sputtering. "You thief! I'll have you arrested…"

The object of his wrath just winked and sat down.

Miri Pat nodded toward her brother. "William, you have the floor. Speak slowly so both uncle and nephew can understand."

Dash covered his laugh with a cough.

William moved the side of the desk next to Tater. He spread out the legal documents. Picking each one up, he read it to Tater, then explained in detail what it meant.

"Do you know what you can and cannot do? Now and forever? Please tell us, so we are all sure there will be no future misunderstanding."

Tater's red face grew redder. "I can go to church, and I can visit Uncle Del, but I can't come into the motherhouse. So I can't visit Annalise in her office or stop in the dining room." He frowned. "Doesn't seem fair. I didn't do all that much, and I said I was sorry I dropped that lady doctor on her head. She shouldn't have squirmed so much."

"Shut up, Tater. Don't admit anything," his uncle said.

Billy raised his eyes to heaven, thinking that boat was already in the middle of the ocean by now.

Dash remained a silent audience.

Sister Miriam Patrice asked, "Mr. Boone, Delmar, do you understand the terms of the restraining order and the no trespass? You don't fully comprehend how upsetting to the sisters your antics were. And I call them yours, because I'm positive you are behind all this."

Delmar mumbled about being blamed for everything and anything that went wrong around here.

"That's not true. You're only being blamed for everything that you set in motion," Sister said.

"I didn't take that toy, and I didn't tell Stupid here to grab some woman. All I did was suggest one or two things. Annalise and Tater did the rest."

"As I told your niece earlier, you should choose your compatriots wisely. Neither of you did that." She stepped around to the front of the desk. Handing Tater copies of the orders, she said, "These are for you to keep and re-read as often as you like. In fact, I encourage it. And I'd like you to initial and date my copies, again, just for the record."

She then moved to Delmar Boone. Leaning on the desk, she asked, "When was the last time you read the agreement you signed when you moved into your apartment? I get the feeling that you think you were given the right to dismiss all the rules and regulations of the apartment complex."

Delmar frowned. "Don't know what you're talking about. I drew up the plans for those apartments, and part of my payment was a guaranteed residence for life. You can't kick me out. It says so in the lease." He crossed his arms to punctuate the last statement with a so-there attitude.

"William, you have the floor once again," she said as she returned to her seat.

Billy again reached into his briefcase. "Mr. Boone, I'm not sure where you got the idea that you could never be evicted from the apartment. There are several clauses at the end of the agreement. Let's call them the fine print."

He handed Delmar a copy where the fine print was now in 28-point font. Easy to read without one's glasses on.

"My sister, bless her, is a very kind, trusting woman. Me, her little brother, not so much. I drew up this contract with these points in mind, since I just had a funny feeling that you would try as hard as you could to skirt the parameters of the document. See Point Four. It basically says that if you break the rules, like smoking in your room or possessing a firearm, you could be evicted."

Delmar started to protest.

Holding up his hand, Billy continued, "Yes, yes, there was a monetary amount set for the work you did on this project, and your rent was subtracted from this amount month by month. In twenty minutes, I can give you a dollar amount owed to you, but it is possible that you might owe them rent. You set the rates, so it won't be too hard to calculate all this."

He handed the document to Delmar. "If you don't believe me, have your own attorney go over this. He or she should have pointed this out to you back then. Mr. Boone, I do believe our business here is finished. But please heed these words: if I discover you are harassing any of the good sisters, I will bury you."

Delmar shook his head. "Hey, Rambo, you got anything to add? Like I'm shaking in my boots. Hearing you cock that pistol, whoa, had trouble sleeping after that little gag. And for the record, I didn't tell Annalise to steal that toy or for Dumbo here to mess with your wife. He was supposed to surprise her, scare her, that's all." Delmar stood and stuffed all the papers into his pocket. "I'm going and I'll stay out of everybody's way. Nice doing business with you, Sister. You'll go broke without me, just you wait."

He wheeled his nephew out of the room, making a point of slamming the door.

Dash started laughing.

"What?" asked Billy.

"I don't know. Right there at the end I thought he might break out into song like Eliza Doolittle, 'Just you wait, Henry Higgins.'"

"Now who is coming up with nonsense?"

"Ah, it's one of Mae and Dolly's fav musicals. Must have heard it a million times over the years. Those two get together and songs will be sung. Someday you should hang around with my sister," Dash said. He turned to Miri Pat. "I must say I'm impressed with the way you managed the Boone men. I was getting nervous just being in the same room."

Billy shook his head. "And, Rambo, where is that mighty weapon of yours? And just in case you're wondering, I'm talking about the sidearm."

Laughing, Dash said, "I left it with Irma. She was holding it until this meeting was over."

Miri Pat motioned for the men to sit while she pulled open the bottom drawer and put the Irish whiskey on the desk. She fumbled around and found three glasses. After pouring two fingers of the golden liquid into the tumblers, she slid them over to Dash and Billy.

"Here's to the McCafferty/Hammond team. Always and forever!"

After downing the whiskey, the trio stood, very pleased with themselves about to head to the dining hall.

Opening the door, Dash walked straight into Sister Annalise and Sister Bernadette.

"Beg pardon," Dash said as he stepped aside.

Annalise shook her head. "No, Colonel, it is I who needs to beg your pardon. I am so sorry for the pain I've caused your family, literally and figuratively. Never did I mean to hurt anyone. I just wanted you to go away and leave me to deal with Miriam Patrice. Please tell your wife and son I'm very sorry."

It was Dash's turn to shake his head. "Sister, the best apologies are delivered in person. The whole family will be in the hall tonight, so stop by and talk to Mae and T.J. Of the two, my wife will be the most forgiving. The four-year-old will lecture you on behaving properly. I know; that's what I hear from him all the time." He moved past her, saying good evening.

Billy waited in the office for the sisters to enter. "Miri Pat, we'll wait in the hall unless you think I'm needed."

"No, William, you go on. Thank you," said Miriam Patrice. She motioned for the sisters to come in and take a seat.

CHAPTER THIRTY-THREE

Dash tracked down his wife and child. The little one was hard at work on a card for Miss Victoria. With furrowed brow and tongue between his teeth, T.J. labored to get the picture right.

"Look, daddy, this is me and Pansy Pup. Just like Miss Victoria and her dog, Lady. Do you think she'll like it?"

"She'll love it. Mommy and I will expect handmade cards from you from now on." Dash tousled his son's hair, then bent down to kiss Mae's cheek.

"How'd it go with Tater and his uncle?" Mae asked.

"Miri Pat was at her finest doing a splendid imitation of the fierce principal. Delmar is on his last warning. Legal eagle William read the fine print in the lease which upset Delmar's applecart. He thought he could be here forever, but Miri Pat and her brother drew up a lease that said otherwise. Delmar really needs to have someone read these legal documents to him, so he knows when shit is heading his way. I think Delmar will be on his best behavior for a bit, and then get booted out for smoking or drinking or both."

T.J. looked up. "Daddy, you're not supposed to say that word. You know if Auntie Re heard you, she'd wash your mouth out again."

Dash looked at a laughing Mae. "Delmar isn't the only one who needs better relatives. I took that nonsense once from Marie to teach T.J. a lesson. Won't happen again."

Billy slid into a chair. "Once again, fly on the wall. I

hoped to stay but this is official community business." He reached over to look at the card T.J. was coloring. "Say, buddy, this is good. Make one for your old Uncle Silly Billy, will you?"

T.J. held out his hand. "One at a time, Uncle Billy. This is really hard work."

"How about ice cream all around? A bit of celebration for a job well done," Billy said as he moved toward the machine. Mae joined him so she could help bring the cones back to the table. For once, T.J. didn't devour his treat. He moved his crayons and the card to the side to avoid any drips.

"Say, cousin mine, that was a cool trick with the bullets. When did you lift them?" asked Billy.

"Bullets? What went on in there?" asked Mae.

"Delmar the dumb brought a weapon to the meeting. His mind must be gone, not going. Did he honestly think we would all crumble and give in once he flashed his weapon?"

Billy raised his hand. "I would in a minute. Coward, not Patrick, is my middle name."

Mae leaned back to study her husband. "So, Colonel Hammond, did you bring your weapon to the meeting? And to repeat Billy's question, when did you lift the bullets?"

"When I toured his apartment, planting the bugs, I opened a drawer and there was the weapon and a box of ammo. Emptied it but for one cartridge and pocketed the box and the loose cartridges, hence no need for me to carry. Besides, the day I can't take a guy like Delmar is the day I will lock myself up in a closet for the rest of my life." Dash finished his cone in one bite. "One cartridge doesn't count for much these days."

Mae rolled her eyes. "Think we should make a poster for the E.R. that spouts that wisdom. The bullet only counts if you're the one it's inside. Sometimes, I wonder how you made it home in one piece."

They all turned to see Miri Pat and Annalise walking toward them.

Annalise nodded to Mae. "Could I speak with you in private for a moment? And T.J.?"

Mother and son walked with Annalise to a quiet corner where it was obvious to onlookers that she was apologizing for her sins. Mae hugged her, but T.J. was having none of it.

"You should know better than to play tricks on little kids. Jesus isn't going to like that. My uncle Sammy is a sheriff, and he would arrest you for that. It's a good thing he didn't come along with Auntie Re," he said as he walked away.

"I'm sorry, Annalise, but he's a Hammond, and forgiveness is a just a very tiny part of their DNA. I hope you and Miriam Patrice came to an agreement. The life you have here is precious; don't throw it away for someone else's dream, especially a man's dream," Mae said.

Annalise excused herself, heading to the church to ask forgiveness for her sins.

Miriam Patrice gave only the slightest recap of the discussion with Annalise. "Let's leave it at she sees the error of her ways, is ready to step back in line and, as suggested, I'm asking her to enroll in a course or two on finance and investing. If she wants to make good decisions, she'll need the proper background." She asked, "Anyone ready for another cone?"

After Billy fetched one for her, she turned to Dash. "What about the good news I dismissed a while ago? Sorry but I find I can only concentrate on one thing at a time."

"No probs, Miri Pat. Your intrepid team of treasure hunters did find the jewels," Dash said smugly.

Miri Pat sat up straight. "Really, where? Where are they now? Dare I hope they'll be worth all this trouble?"

Mae shook her head. "Sorry, Miri Pat, but they are worth quite a bit. While the three of you were berating the Boones, Sister Agnes Marie, Thomas, and I were brainstorming. Here's the gist of the plan: Sister will author a book about the Harris family with all its moles and warts. Then, with the cooperation of the more artistic sisters, a small display of Harris family belongings will be exhibited. The jewels on busts of Mrs. Harris and Victoria. Agnes Marie thinks there might be some old dresses and bonnets in the attic. If not, I'm sure the talented seamstresses among you can whip up a period costume or two. The front room will become a mini museum complete with gift shop, selling Agnes Marie's book and souvenir postcards of the stained-glass windows in the Reading Room and elsewhere on this beautiful campus."

Dash and Billy just smiled.

"You thought of that, Maevis," Dash said. "It's positively brilliant. A tour of the grounds, maybe even a ghost walk." He turned to Miri Pat. "You're going to need a publicity director ..."

Mae held up her hand. "Hold on, Buster. You aren't going to be here to supervise or have anything to do with this. This is a project for the sisters. Something to rejuvenate them. You are going home to run your own bookstore."

Before she could finish, Dash nodded. "Yes, yes, we'll stock Agnes Marie's book and those postcards. First step in nationwide distribution." He pulled out his phone and began texting wildly.

"See what you started? After all these years of being around him and yet you've learned nothing. He's going to drive us and the good sisters crazy following up on everything. The man who wouldn't cross the Ohio River will be camping out here. Maevis, Maevis," Billy said sadly.

Dash looked around the table. "You are right, all of you. I'll put all this out of my mind. Let's get back to finishing here and heading home. Things to do there, my lovelies."

Mae and Billy just looked at each other, making the sign of the Cross with a silent prayer.

Billy whispered to Mae, "Sure there isn't a pill for this?"

She smiled, "It's called cyanide."

CHAPTER THIRTY-FOUR

After a suitable time for visiting, Dash could feel himself getting antsy. In his mind it was time to pack up and prepare for the trip home. Finally, he could wait no longer, so he stood and announced, "This has been wonderful, but if we are going to head home tomorrow, I suggest we begin to gather and pack our belongings. We'll head out as soon as there is sufficient light so we can see any ice on the highway."

The final discussion was to determine who would drive which car and who would ride with whom. Once that was settled, everyone moved to begin packing.

"All your suitcases, bags, and junk should be in the reception area no later than seven. We can grab a box of cereal and drinks. Billy and I will load the cars, and then we're off," Dash said. "Now, sleeping arrangements for tonight. Billy, Mae, T.J., and I will be in the Reading Room so we can say goodbye to Miss Victoria. Marie, you'll be upstairs, so set an alarm. Text me if you need help with your bags; I don't remember which were yours and which belonged to the Tydie sisters. Lordy, but that seems years ago, not days."

Mae instructed T.J. to give good night kisses all around, then took his hand and all his art paraphernalia. "We're off to gather our stuff. Okay if I bring it all to the Reading Room?"

Dash ended the night with one last walk around with Sister Miriam Patrice and Jumbo.

The Reading Room was quiet when he crept in to go to

bed. A soft light was glowing from the rocking chair.

Dash nodded at the light and whispered, "Good night, Miss Victoria."

CHAPTER THIRTY-FIVE

The trip home was uneventful, just the way Dash wanted it. After dropping Billy off in Columbus, the caravan of two cars headed north to Clover Pointe.

They alerted Grandpa to the probable arrival time so he and the dogs were standing on the front porch waiting as the family pulled in.

T.J. tore out of his car seat, towing his backpack. He struggled with the car door, but Grandpa stepped in to help open it.

"Grandpa, Grandpa, I have so much to tell you, and so much to show you."

"Well, Thomas, come on in," Owen said to his grandson. To his son and daughter-in-law, he said, "Listen, Annie brought over dinner. I just have to put it in the oven about an hour out from when you want to eat. Any idea when that will be?"

Dash shook his head. "Right now, I want to take a long hot shower and get into my sweats, maybe stretch out on the bed for a few minutes."

"Yes, that's what you should do, and Mae should wash your back. Head on upstairs and I'll call you when the dinner is ready, say in an hour, hour and a half."

Dash looked at Mae and smiled. He grabbed her hand, starting for the stairs. "Quick before he changes his mind. An hour to ourselves. I must have been a good boy."

She returned his smile. "Let's see just how good you can be …"

The alarm on Dash's watch buzzed waking him from his nap. He rolled over and kissed Mae's cheek. "Time to get up, sweetheart. Dinner will be ready."

She mumbled something that sounded like 'sure, in a minute.'

Dash listened at the top of the stairs. He could make out his father snoring and the little guy as well. Tiptoeing down to the living room, he found his father and his son curled up in the recliner, T.J.'s artwork spread around the chair.

He reached down to collect the papers and found a card with a drawing of one of the Reading Room windows, the one where Victoria is a young girl and has Lady sleeping by her side. He studied the card for a minute. Very good likeness to the window. He opened it and found a message written inside. The handwriting was graceful and flowing. For a minute, he thought he recognized it as that of the old will T.J. and Mae studied in the main hall of the motherhouse. Shaking his head, he wondered which old sister made the card so T.J. would have a souvenir.

Flipping the card over, he read: Thomas, always believe, Love, Victoria.

He set the card on the fireplace mantel. As he walked away, he returned to it.

Reading it again, he said to himself, 'maybe I will, Miss Victoria, maybe I will.'

ABOUT THE AUTHOR

Elaine Munsch, a native of Cleveland, Ohio, has divided her adult life between that state and Kentucky. She graduated from Nazareth College of Kentucky located outside of Bardstown, and close to her maternal grandfather's home in Balltown. She attended The Ohio State University doing work for a Masters in English Literature. In 1972, she embarked on her life-long passion, that of bookselling. In 1995, she moved from Cleveland to Louisville to open the first Barnes & Noble in Kentucky. She set up a mystery reading group, taught classes in the mystery genre for the Veritas Society and joined the local chapter of Sisters in Crime.

With Susan Bell, she co-edited Mystery with a Splash of Bourbon, an anthology of bourbon-related crime stories for the chapter.

She writes the Dash Hammond series set on the shores of Lake Erie. A HAUNTING AT MARIANWOOD is the sixth book in this series.